Princess Nevermore

Princess Nevermore

~

by Dian Curtis Regan

Cataloging-in-Publication

Regan, Dian Curtis.
Princess Nevermore / by Dian Curtis Regan. —[Updated and expanded ed.]
      p. ; cm.
ISBN-13: 978-1-58196-055-6
ISBN-10: 1-58196-055-7
Sequel: Cam's quest.—When a fifteen-year-old Mandrian princess makes a wish in a wizard's circle, she winds up on Outer Earth and without the ability and desire to return home.
1. Princesses—Juvenile fiction. 2. Wishes—Juvenile fiction. [1. Princesses—Fiction. 2. Wishes—Fiction. 3. Fantasy.] I. Title.
PZ7.R25854 Pr 2007
[Fic] dc22
OCLC: 71201689

Published by Darby Creek Publishing,
a division of Oxford Resources, Inc.
7858 Industrial Parkway
Plain City, OH 43064
www.darbycreekpublishing.com

Printed in the United States of America

2 4 6 8 10 9 7 5 3 1

For Jodi Koumalats, a.k.a. Jodi Thomas,
and
Dewanna Pace, a.k.a. Dia Hunter,
who've always believed
in magic and Mandrian truths

～

ACKNOWLEDGEMENTS

I'd like to thank Tanya Dean and the good folks at
Darby Creek Publishing for making *Princess
Nevermore* available to readers once again and for the
opportunity to update and expand the text that I
began writing when I was barely out of my teens.

Special thanks to all the readers who wrote to ask,
"What happens next?" The story of Princess
Nevermore and the wizard's apprentice continues in
the novel, *Cam's Quest*.
It's a Mandrian truth.

~

Contents

1

The Wishing Pool

~

Princess Quinn of the underground Kingdom of Mandria steadied herself as she balanced upon a footstool in the circle of light directly below the wishing pool.

On the upper side of the pool, in the outer world, a footbridge arched above the water. On the crest of the bridge, a maiden stood, eyes closed, muttering a wish from deep within her heart.

Curious, the princess tilted her head and strained to hear the wishing words.

"Spying on unsuspecting folk is not fitting behavior for the future queen of Mandria," chided the wizard, Melikar.

His voice broke Quinn's concentration. As she turned to answer, her foot slipped off the stool, making her tumble onto the cobbled rock floor of the only chamber in all of the underground kingdoms where the two worlds came together.

Disappointed at the loss of the moment, Quinn wrinkled her nose at Melikar, who'd turned away, probably to hide his amusement at the consequence of her "unfitting behavior."

A coin plunked to the rock floor. Now it was her turn to be amused. A long-ago spell, cast by the wizard, kept water from splashing down into the highest chamber in the castle. The enchantment maintained the pool's stillness, creating a window to the other world. Yet, coins fell through the spell. This annoyed Melikar, as well as Cam, the wizard's apprentice, whose job it was to sweep the coins away.

"I do not know what fascinates you and Cam about folk in the outer world," Melikar said. "They seem an unhappy lot, coming to the pool all hours, wanting this and wanting that. Some wish with such intensity, they wake me in the middle of the night. I've half a mind to conjure myself a proper roof."

Gathering up the many skirts of her sapphire gown, Quinn scrambled to her feet. His words alarmed her. "Sire, please do not remove the pool from view."

Visiting the wizard's chamber to dream about the other world was one of few joys remaining in the princess's life. Her days of tarrying about the castle, having adventures with Cam—or Ameka, her tutor—were drawing to a close.

By Mandrian law, a princess must choose a husband

before her sixteenth birthday. After that, her days would be a series of have-to-dos, filled with royal protocol. Her life would be a book already set forth.

It was a Mandrian truth, and Mandrian truths could not be argued. To Quinn, the law sounded wearisome, tedious, and dull.

The wizard set a lighted candle in a spiked holder on his workbench and resumed mixing a concoction to soothe the king's sore muscles—a consequence of living in the damp underground world. He sprinkled rue, wild yam, and pure gold dust into a flask.

The princess wandered the chamber while waiting to deliver the flask to her father. Shadows flickered mysteriously against rounded walls. Furnishings included ornately carved herb cabinets, tables, and chairs, crafted for the wizard by Marnies in their bustling village below the main avenues of the kingdom.

Marnies tended the gardens, orchards, and wild game areas. The small creatures, covered with fur from head to hoof, the same color as the gold they mined, supplied the underground kingdom with most of its needs: candles, furnishings, and food.

Quinn stopped near the hearth and gazed into the fire, wishing she could "read the flames" the way Melikar did. Sometimes he told her and Cam of details he saw in the other world: Great bodies of water one could not swim across. White-capped mountain peaks set against blue skies. Mighty cities and isolated villages. The coldness of snow in winter; the warmth of sun in summer. The taste of rain and the beauty of the earth preparing for winter-death.

These stories only filled the princess with more desire to see it for herself—and soon, before it became too late.

The wizard popped a cork atop the flask and handed it to Quinn. As her fingers curved around the warm glass, a great whirring noise and spark of brilliant light knocked her once more to the cold, rock floor.

The flashy commotion was the materialization of Cam.

He gaped at the princess, then whirled to see where he was. "Bats!" Cam exclaimed, peering at the magic ring he'd been trying to create with his limited enchanter's ability. "The ring was supposed to take me to the Marnie village to fetch candles, not here. I twisted it three times and pictured exactly where I wanted to go."

"Candles were clearly not the object of your thoughts," Melikar muttered, glancing from his apprentice to the disarrayed princess.

Quinn gathered her skirts a second time and came to her feet. "That ring is clearly the master, and you are its slave." She straightened and smoothed her gown. "Ay, the lace is torn."

Cam looked so forlorn, the princess wished she hadn't spoken harshly. He'd worked diligently on the ring after she'd teased him about his magical failures. Softening her voice, she added. "Don't worry, I won't tell the queen—"

"Devil dust!"

Quinn and Cam both flinched at the wizard's outburst. Obviously, the interruption was annoying him.

"Recast the spell, lad, and look it up in the Book to make sure you get it right this time. It needn't take three twists to make the magic work."

The princess returned to dusting her gown, lowering her voice to appease the wizard. "You could have appeared on the *other* side of the chamber or simply *walked* through the door like a normal Mandrian."

When Cam did not respond, she glanced at him to see why. The startled look on his face told her he wasn't listening.

Melikar's comment sank in. He'd given his apprentice permission to open the Mandrian Book of Magic. Cam had never been allowed to touch it. All the magic known to enchanters was in the Book. If Cam had not caused such a disturbance while the wizard was busy, Quinn was certain Melikar would have looked up the spell himself.

Cam caught her eye. The two had discussed traveling to the outer world many times—merely for a day's sojourn. The anticipation of wondrous adventures awaiting them thrilled the princess.

Melikar would never allow it, of course. Neither would King Marit or Queen Leah, who were quite protective of their only daughter, heir to the Mandrian throne.

The princess nodded at the apprentice. She knew his thoughts matched hers, as often they did. Now that the Book lay open before him, it would be quite simple to locate the proper spell.

Cam stepped across the chamber to the oak stand that held the book. Quinn noticed the trembling of his hand as he turned the pages. Perhaps she should distract the wizard before he noted how long the search was taking his apprentice.

"Sire?" she began. "Has any Mandrian ever traveled to the other world?"

Melikar studied her over the candle flame. "Why, child?"

"Shouldn't someone go and inform the folk who plead with us for wishes that we cannot grant them?" She kept one eye on Cam, whose lanky form curved over the Book. Dark hair hung long, almost covering his eyes as he mumbled magic words to the ring.

Melikar's eyes glinted blood-red in the flickering light. "They're not asking us to fulfill their wishes; they do not know we are here."

Behind the wizard, Cam moved to the cauldron bubbling upon the hearth. Picking up a ladle, he began to stir the brew.

Puzzled, Quinn wondered why he would abandon the Book and return to his chores. Why let this jolly opportunity slip through his fingers? *Their* fingers.

"Perhaps then," the princess continued, "Cam and I could journey beyond the pool to inform folk not to depend upon the wishing pool for answers." Quinn absently twisted her lion-colored braid, which had been growing for all of her fifteen years.

"Princess," Melikar responded in a firm voice, "for no reason can you leave Mandria. Whether or not I can send you is another matter. Folk in the other world are different from us. If they discovered where you came from, they'd descend on us with shovels and dig up our rooftops."

"But—"

"Enough," spoke the wizard.

An elder's words could not be argued. It was a Mandrian truth, yet sometimes Quinn needed to be reminded.

The wizard pointed a bony finger at her. "There is no magic in the other world. Centuries ago, enchanted creatures were driven to the underground kingdoms. Cam would not endure long there."

Though absorbed by the wizard's tale, Quinn's eyes were drawn to the wishing pool. The water had begun to swirl in a wide circle.

She tried not to react while Melikar was looking at her, but the sight was stunning. Never before had she seen the water so much as ripple.

The wizard, hunched over his workbench, did not notice the oddity. "It takes magic in one's surroundings to make the magic inside work," he told her. "Cam would weaken as his magic faded. If he did not return to Mandria within a short time, he would die."

The princess glanced at Cam, who was not listening to the wizard's warning. She'd inform him of this later and make sure their journey lasted but a day.

"That," Melikar was saying, "is why our kingdom abounds with enchanted creatures." He leaned toward her, eyes wide, and whispered, "The middle of the earth holds magic."

A sudden knock at the door drew Melikar from his workbench. Quinn was grateful for the further distraction. Her own attention remained fixed upon the pool. She moved toward it, drawn as if beckoned by a spell.

The faster Cam stirred the brew in the cauldron, the faster the water swirled.

Transfixed, the princess stepped into the circle of light beneath the pool. At the same moment, Cam whisper-chanted:

> *"Anger, fear, love, and mirth.*
> *Send Quinn and Cam to Outer Earth."*

2

A Forbidden Spell

A scream broke Cam's focus as he hunched over the cauldron, chanting.

He whirled about to see what was happening. Misty fog encircled the princess as she stood in the circle of light beneath the wishing pool.

Holy bats! The spell is working!

Dropping the ladle, he raced to join her—and promptly tripped over the footstool. Sprawling on the floor, he gawked at the thick mist and the turbulent water swirling above him.

There was no sign of the princess. She was gone. Disappeared into the fog.

Cam looked down at his body, thrilled with anticipation. Was he disappearing into the mist as well? *Toads and mugwort! This is fantastic!*

"Get up!" shouted Melikar.

But . . . if the spell is working, the wizard should not be able to see—

"Cam!"

The truth hit him like a mudslide in the grotto.

The spell took the princess—but not him.

I'm still here, below the wishing pool.

Bats!

Afraid to meet Melikar's eyes, Cam reached for the magic ring with frantic plans of making a fast escape.

On second thought, staying to take the blame seemed more honorable—which was just as well, since he'd dropped the ring when he raced to the circle. He'd search for it later.

The wizard helped him to his feet with a quick yank. "Do you know what you've done?"

Cam stood as tall as he could on trembling legs, straightened his tunic, and faced his master. "I'm truly sorry," he said. And he was, for he'd hoped to travel with Quinn to the other world. "Can you bring her back now?"

"Bring her back?" Melikar looked aghast at the suggestion. "I cannot bring her back until she *chooses* to return." He gave his apprentice a red-eyed glare. "The difficulty is—she does not know this."

Cam took the whole burden upon his heart. *What have I done?* He trudged in a circle, mumbling to himself about the ring, the spell, and the question of why he had not gone with the princess after he'd chanted both their names.

The princess.

Alone in the other world—without him to protect her.

Fear for her safety, as well as fear for his very life when the king learned of his careless deed, made him fall to his knees.

"Master, you must punish me. You've been good to take me in, give me food to eat, and a cot on which to sleep." Bowing his head to avoid Melikar's displeased scrutiny, he continued, "Then I repay you with disobedience. I do not deserve to be your apprentice."

The wizard placed a shaky hand upon Cam's shoulder. "Your prank was a thoughtless one indeed, but the tapestry has been woven and the thread, snipped."

Melikar tightened his grip to quell his anger. "You were not taken with the princess because you were not beneath the pool when the spell was cast. Once I've spoken the words allowing her to return, she must be standing atop the footbridge, directly over the pool.

"She must wish with all her heart to come home, then pivot to set the whirlpool in motion—the same way you created one by stirring the liquid in the cauldron. As the water begins to swirl, she will be drawn into it—as long as she does not resist the magic." Melikar released his hold on Cam. "That is the only way Mandria's princess can return to her kingdom."

"She'll come back," Cam said, more to reassure himself than Melikar. "She may explore a little first, but—"

"This is what I fear."

Melikar studied the pool, but nothing was discernible through the now-cloudy water. "The spell to return can be cast but once and is strong for only a quarter-moon's turn."

Cam's breathing stopped with the wizard's words. "That is only a few days."

The wizard's answer was a solemn nod.

The apprentice came to his feet. If he had not acted so rashly, he would have read all of this in the Book and discussed it fully with Quinn before impulsively conjuring her out of Mandria.

Melikar moved to the stand that held the Book and opened it gently. "I've been wise not to let you touch this. I trusted you were ready, but you've shown me it's still too soon."

Cam felt as disheartened as he had on the day he'd asked Melikar about his parents and learned he'd been abandoned—left for the wizard to raise.

He was a nobody without a past—and with little promise for a future as an enchanter if he was never allowed to open the Mandrian Book of Magic.

It seemed he spent all of his time trying to prove he was responsible—to earn Melikar's trust and Quinn's affection. But if mistakes were gold pieces, he would truly be a wealthy lad.

The ring.

The question of why he'd appeared here instead of in the Marnie Village suddenly became clear to him. He'd been thinking about the princess—not about candles.

Ay, there was nothing wrong with the spell he'd cast on the ring. It was *his* fault. He supposed if Quinn had been in the Marnie Village, he might have been more successful.

Melikar moved to his workbench as though the weight of both worlds was on his shoulders. He gathered a clean bowl and flask. "Fetch me a dish of snake root, stinging nettle, doleran seeds—"

Cam's gasp caused the wizard to pause. "But, Sire, doleran seeds will stop a . . . a life."

"Not a life, lad. Time. The seeds, steeped in the royal tea, will make time stand still for the king and queen until their daughter returns. *If* she returns." He muttered the last part under his breath, but the words burned Cam's ears.

The king and queen had already taken afternoon tea so the plan would have to wait until morning.

Heart pounding, the apprentice searched the oak cabinet for doleran seeds. *How can Melikar chance something like this?*

As if he'd read Cam's thoughts, Melikar replied, "Do you have a better course of action? If King Marit discovers that his beloved daughter and heir to the throne is missing on my account, he'll have both our heads."

Cam swallowed hard. The wizard had spoken the truth. A reply was unnecessary.

Hearing Melikar take the blame made Cam feel even worse. Meekly he asked, "Is there anything else we can do?"

The wizard's eyes suddenly dimmed to a watery red. "I will search the Book for any spell I can cast from below the river to ensure Quinn's safety, should she rashly decide to remain in the outer world."

The horrid thought of the princess—*his* princess, his childmate, his confidante—remaining in the other world without him, saddened Cam far more than not knowing who he was or from whence he came.

3

The Other Side

$\mathcal{I}$n her dream, the princess lifted the lace skirt of her sapphire gown and stepped down the spiral rock stairway descending from Melikar's chamber. She found her way down countless corridors and stairways until she arrived in the courtyard.

Beyond the castle gate, Quinn hurried along Mandria's main avenue, following its winding curves through the kingdom, dodging horse-drawn carriages and knights on handsome stallions.

Enchanted daylight, conjured by Melikar, lit the underground world, peaking at mid-day, then gradually growing dimmer until evening. It seemed a poor imitation of the brightness the princess had glimpsed above the wishing pool, but this was the world she had always known.

Shops along the way glowed warmly, lit by Marnie candles. Quinn was tempted to dawdle and see what new items had arrived from other kingdoms. The weavers of Banyyan always sent the best silk, and bakers in Twickingham were known for their lavish creations of sweets.

But her dream journey seemed urgent. It was imperative that she arrive at Ameka's cottage at once, yet the princess was unsure of the reason.

Turning down the last tunnel along the way, Quinn fairly ran to the cottage at the end of the lane and vigorously rapped upon the door.

She waited, expecting Ameka to fling open the portal and draw her in, yet the door never opened. Her tutor was not home.

Quinn's heartbeat quickened. If Ameka were not present, then it meant . . .

I'm all by myself. Completely alone.

A moment later, the cottage began to grow hazy and disappear. Shouting for Ameka, the princess pounded on the oak door, but in two raps her hand went right through the place where the thick plank had been.

Quinn's eyes flew open as she awoke from the dream.

Instantly she blinked them shut.

The brightness of the fiery sun was remarkably intense. Cupping one hand over her eyes, she sat up, squinting into the glow, feeling its warmth for the very first time.

Dizziness fuzzed her head, making her feel as

though she'd just danced the quick-stepping volta in the Great Hall with her cousin, Dagon.

Steadying herself, she kept her eyes half-closed against the painful brightness surrounding her. *Where am I?*

The last few moments slowly came to her. *Cam's spell! Had it worked?*

Glancing about, the princess realized she was sitting upon a curved wooden footbridge. Beneath the bridge, blue-green water sparkled in the light, like jewels in her father's crown.

Quinn could scarcely breathe. The wishing pool was *below* her! Her heart soared. For once, the apprentice's magic did what it was supposed to do.

Feeling weak in spite of the excitement—or because of it—the princess grasped the railing and pulled herself to her feet. The thrill was the same she'd felt the first time she'd been allowed to visit Melikar's chamber—and had caught her earliest glimpse of the world above the river. A world whispered about in nursery fables among lads and lasses who believed it a faery tale, while at the same time, wishing it were true.

Well, it is true. And here I am!

Cam must have sent her up through the water, yet her gown was not even damp. All she remembered was being drawn to the pool. A tingling sensation had swept over her with such force, its subtle beckoning had become an urgent demand.

She'd heard Cam chant. Then an earthquake had

rumbled through her head. What happened after that was hazy.

Cam. Where is he?

Quinn turned in a circle, searching for the apprentice, who was nowhere in sight. Was he playing a trick on her? Now was *not* the time for such foolishness.

"*Cam!*" she called. "Show yourself this instant." Her voice sounded weak and thin with no walls and tunnels to echo it back to her.

She stood transfixed, captivated by the scene that had always been out of her view from below the river. A lush forest surrounded her. A path came out of the forest on one side, over the bridge, then crossed a clearing and wound its way back into the trees.

No Outer-Earth folk were in sight. Still, Quinn hurried off the footbridge and into the shadowed forest, just to be safely out of view. Here, shade from looming trees was gentler on her eyes.

Now the only thing to do was find a good sitting spot and wait for Cam to appear. *He has to. I heard him say both our names when the spell was cast.*

Inhaling one long breath after another, Quinn wandered into the forest, sampling fragrances all new to her.

Finding a boulder within clear view of the footbridge, she sat to wait. If Cam did not appear soon, surely Melikar would materialize in a lightning flash on top of the footbridge, amber robes flapping about him like wings, and rescue her with a great display of magic.

As excited as she was about being in this world,

the fearful fluttering of her heart told her she did not want to miss what might be her only chance to return to Mandria.

Minutes passed. Nothing happened.

Quinn recalled Melikar's warning: *The outer world isn't safe for enchanted beings.* Luckily or unluckily, she was an ordinary, unenchanted princess.

"Toads and mugwort," she grumbled. Now her voice sounded small and trembly. She and Cam always planned on taking this adventure together. Neither had suggested she do it by herself.

A foggy remembrance of her dream journey to Ameka's cottage washed over her. Was it truly a dream? Or a forewarning?

Panic flushed her neck. In Mandria, she was rarely alone—not with her two ladies, Cydlin and Gwynell, attending her. Cam or Ameka took up the rest of her time—or Dagon, whenever he and her uncle, Lord Ryswick, came to visit from Twickingham.

The princess hugged herself, wishing she'd brought along a traveling cape. Her gown was no protection from the cool breeze, gusting like the wind drafts out by Oxbury Falls. "I'm truly alone," she said.

"I'm here," came a tiny voice from behind.

Quinn leaped to her feet. All she saw was an ancient tree with gold and red leaves rustling in the breeze. "Who is there?" She twisted her braid through her fingers, taking a wary step backward. "Show yourself at once."

"Look here," said the voice.

At the base of the tree, amid gnarly roots, the misty form of a maiden—no taller than a Marnie's knee—shifted like a candle flame.

The sight stunned the princess. Did Melikar not tell her that all magical creatures lived underground?

"Are you an enchantress?" the wispy maiden asked. "Hundreds of years ago, we could move and talk, but when magic left the earth, we became still and mute. Yet you—" She pointed at Quinn. "You are surrounded with magic."

Fascinated, Quinn knelt for a better look. The outline of the maiden's smoky form shifted with every gust of the breeze. "No, I'm not an enchantress," Quinn told her. "Magic is common where I live, and—"

The princess stopped, remembering her promise to keep Mandria a secret. "Um, perhaps a little has rubbed off on me."

Another form appeared, floating above a lily of the valley like a wisp of steam.

Tiny maidens emerged one by one from the plants and trees nearest her. The moment she walked away, Quinn assumed they'd disappear into their living homes, frozen once again. "I cannot make it last," she told them. "I'm sorry."

Remembering who she was, the princess returned to her rock throne, straightening the torn lace on her gown. She was here as an ambassador from her kingdom; she must act accordingly.

"Who are you?" she asked the maidens. "And why

were you not taken when magic left the earth?"

"We're dryads," answered a figure floating above a patch of tansy. "Wood nymphs. Moving to the underground kingdoms was impossible because our homes are here. Melikar had to leave us behind."

"Melikar?" Hearing the wizard's name startled Quinn so much, she came to her feet. "How do you know of Melikar?"

The nymphs old enough to remember told Quinn of the time when Earth was filled with magical creatures. They told how men began to capture spirits, turning good magic into evil, taking power for their own greedy intentions.

After a time, Earth became unsafe for anyone possessing the gift. So the wizard, Melikar, found a new world for his followers. And, without the surrounding magic, dryads remain frozen in their forest homes.

Although the tale was absorbing, Quinn's attention kept wandering. She could not waste another moment. A whole world awaited her—and she'd better act now before Melikar called her home.

Bidding the maidens good-bye—and apologizing for taking away the magic—she made her way through tall twitchgrass to the footbridge. At the crest of the bridge, she leaned against the handrail and gazed into the wishing pool.

Looking *down* into the water seemed odd after looking *up* through it all her life. Craning her neck, she searched for a glimpse of Melikar's chamber but saw nothing more than her own reflection.

Something glinted in the sparkling water. Hoping it was a sign from below, Quinn dropped to her knees, then realized the shiny reflection came from her side of the pool. Caught on the lacy hem of her gown was a ring—Cam's magic ring!

The ring must have snagged on her skirt, yet she had no idea how or when. Pulling it free, she tried it on. Since it was fitted to Cam's hand, it was too loose for any finger save her middle one.

The sudden sound of voices caught her attention. Across the clearing, three people emerged from the forest and started down the path toward the pool.

Hurrying off the bridge, Quinn lifted her skirts and climbed down a small hill to the bank of the river, where she could hunch out of sight beneath the curve of the bridge.

"Hurry, Sarah!" shouted a lad. "It's almost time for the shuttle to leave."

Quinn peeked.

A maiden, about her age, ran onto the bridge. Closing her eyes, she mumbled softly to herself.

Quinn tried to get a good look and almost splashed into the water. The maiden's fair hair was shorter than a lad's, which made the princess wrinkle her nose. What an oddity. Maidens in Mandria never cut their hair until they became betrothed. It was a Mandrian truth.

Her clothes were unusual: a buttonless shirt with a design on the front and dark leggings like a lad would wear. Trinkets dangled from each ear. Quinn was intrigued and wanted to speak to her.

Halfway across the clearing, an old man stopped next to the lad. "Sarah!" he called. "Come away from the pool!"

The abrupt shout in the quiet forest startled the maiden. Reaching into her pocket, she pulled out a coin, kissed it, then tossed it into the wishing pool.

Quinn imagined Melikar's annoyance as the coin plunked to the floor of his chamber. The image gave her a twinge of homesickness, even though she'd been gone mere minutes.

The lad bounded onto the footbridge. He was taller than Sarah, but with the same coloring.

Quinn's heart quickened. He was as handsome as any knight in Mandria. He even reminded her a little of Dagon.

"Come on, Sis. We'll miss the bus if you don't hurry. Mondo has to get home in time for work."

"But we just got here," she argued. "Why are we leaving already?"

The lad shrugged. "I don't know. Wondered the same thing myself."

Together they started across the clearing where the old man waited.

Quinn's curiosity overflowed, like the marble fountains on the castle green. Scrambling back to the footbridge, she threw a final, hasty glance at the wishing pool—and home—then followed the strangers down the path into the forest.

4

Dragons, Large and Small

❧

Quinn kept her distance from the others on the path. Whenever she slowed, a tingle shivered through her. Was the surrounding magic awakening other wood nymphs in the forest?

Hurrying on, she felt an unexplainable obsession to keep Sarah, the lad, and the old man in view.

The path ended at a gateway. A sign, penned in fancy letters read *"To the Wishing Pool"* with an arrow pointing back the way she'd come.

The scene beyond the gate made Quinn falter. Dozens of folk filled a large open area, moving among gigantic contraptions of the oddest sort. Pray, what was their purpose? Bright, flashing lights pained her eyes. Loud, bouncy music likewise pained her ears.

One of the contraptions was a gigantic sphere with

many swings hanging from it. The swings were filled
with people. As the princess watched, the circle began
its wide turn, carrying swings high into the air, around,
down, then up again. At the top, Outer-Earth folk
screamed and waved their arms.

Another contraption looked like a giant spider, but at
the end of each skinny leg was a basket full of people,
spinning and calling out to each other.

From every direction, shouts and screams seemed
to shake the air. Why were these people being punished? What horrible crimes had they committed?

Quinn's fear made her step behind a fountain to
observe and not be seen. This must be an Outer-Earth
prison. How barbaric! In Mandria the worst punish-
ments were life in a cold, dark dungeon, banishment, or
beheading. They'd done away with torture such as this
centuries ago. It was a Mandrian truth.

Shuddering, her gaze traveled the crowd, searching
for Sarah.

The maiden, lad, and man were about to be swallowed
by the crowd. Taking a deep breath for courage, Quinn
stepped quickly past the horrid contraptions—and past
numerous folk who gave her curious double-glances.

She followed the trio until they came to a giant arch
lit with blinking spots of bright color. *How odd.* Quinn
stepped beneath the arch, then turned to read the
words: *Welcome to WonderLand Park.*

Beyond the arch, she spotted Sarah climbing aboard
a strange machine with large wheels.

Even though the princess did not understand why the notion of losing sight of the family worried her so, she honored the feeling and followed. Catching up her skirts, she rushed past a line of prisoners waiting to enter the torture area and hoped no one mistook her for one of them.

Quinn hesitated a few steps from the monster who'd swallowed Sarah. She could hear it grumbling. Its hunched form reminded her of the great dragons that once roamed this world. A few still bothered the underground kingdoms, but now, small dragons, quick to tame, were fashionable as pets.

Scrabit, her own pet dragon, had come as a birth gift from King Exeter in the Kingdom of Chelwick. She loved Scrabit-sized dragons but did not want this adventure to end by being swallowed by this large, ugly one.

Don't be foolish, her mind chided. *It is not a dragon.*

I know. But it's big and noisy and frightening.

The princess spotted the maiden inside, watching her. She did not appear frightened at all.

"Are ya gittin' on or not?" came a gruff voice from behind her.

Quinn flinched at the rude comment from a burly man. No one ever spoke to royalty like that. The man should be whisked off by palace guards.

Or, would be, if this were Mandria.

Melikar, is this the proper course of action?

Quinn's plea to the wizard brought instant guilt. His true response would be, *"No, the proper course of action is to come home."* Yet, she hoped he was somehow watching over her. Perhaps that explained her urgency to stay with the family who'd come to the wishing pool.

Feeling determined, the princess caught hold of a handrail and pulled herself up the steps. Folk sat facing her, two by two, with an aisle between. She stared at them as they stared back.

The gruff man followed her up the stairs and sat behind a large wheel. "Take a seat; it's time to leave."

His unpleasant tone bothered her. Was he a prison guard? Better not vex him or he might force her onto one of the torture contraptions. Lifting her chin, she proudly returned everyone's stares as she made her way between the rows of chairs.

The old man was sitting next to the lad. Behind them sat Sarah. Quinn chose the empty seat next to her.

"Hey," the girl said, looking Quinn up and down, seeming unable to take her eyes off the sapphire gown and jeweled Mandrian slippers.

Before the princess could return the greeting, the dragon let out a great roar and crept forward. Quinn braced herself, waiting for the machine to spin around, turn upside down, or make her scream.

The dragon simply moved faster.

"Are you okay?" the maiden asked, still gaping at her.

Quinn leaned toward the window to watch as they passed rows and rows of small carriages. "I'm fine, Sarah. Thank you."

Sarah drew back, looking surprised. "How did you

know my name?"

"I overheard your brother calling you."

"Adam?"

At the mention of his name, Adam rose up in the seat in front of her and leaned his elbows against the headrest.

His eyes quickly took in her face, her hair, and her gown. He offered his hand, "Hi. I'm Adam Dover."

In Mandria, no one was allowed to touch royalty, but since he did not know her status, the princess did what a lady of nobility would do. She crooked her wrist and took hold of his fingers, expecting him to bow and kiss her hand. "I'm Quinn," she replied, feeling shy under his scrutiny.

"Quinn what?" He wiggled her hand up and down instead of kissing it.

How odd! How disrespectful!

The princess abruptly drew her hand away. "Quinn of Mandria," she replied, leaving off her title. Telling them the truth might endanger the secret of the underground world. The wizard would never forgive her if she did.

Adam cocked his head, as if puzzled by her answer. He motioned toward the old man. "This is our grand-father, Mondo. We live with him."

Mondo turned, peering at her between the seats with a somber look. "Hello, Quinn," He spoke in a hushed voice, as if he did not want others to hear. "Welcome."

The old man's face startled her.

His gaze was intense; his eyes, a vivid blue-green, the same deep hue as the wishing pool. The contrast of the color against his white hair and beard was striking.

A vague familiarity touched her senses. Had they met before?

And why had he greeted her with "welcome"?

5

Puzzlements and Bewilderments

~

"The dress!" Sarah exclaimed, snapping her fingers. "I just figured out why you're dressed like that. You must be acting in the Shakespeare Festival at WonderLand Park." She grinned, seeming pleased by her conclusion. "Are you a princess?"

The question caught Quinn by surprise. "Yes," she answered, dropping her voice to a whisper. "How did you know?"

Sarah looked at her as though she'd said something doltish. "By your costume, of course. Acting in a play must be really cool."

The princess had no idea what the maiden was talking about or why an actor might be colder than anyone else.

While considering a good answer, Quinn's attention

was drawn beyond the maiden to the passing scenery. The forest gave way to tall castles and cottages, but they were boxy and plain. No turrets. No towers. No draw-bridges.

If folk of this world lacked magic, they also lacked imagination.

The wheeled machine flew past intriguing sights faster than her pony, Trinka, could gallop. In spite of all there was to see, what intrigued the princess most was the sky. The wide openness of this world's "ceiling" was amazing. Just looking at it made her feel light and airy, as if she could float up and touch one of the puffy shapes Melikar called clouds.

The sun seemed to be dropping toward the horizon. Its rays, still bright, cast peculiar-shaped shadows across the land. In two blinks, the brightness slipped from sight, as if a giant's hand had reached up and snatched it away.

Lights began to appear in a multitude of windows, making the princess wonder how large the candle chamber must be to supply all those candles. And who made them? All Marnies lived underground.

Other oddities that captured Quinn's attention were the hundreds of carriages moving by themselves without horses. She even caught a glimpse of the flying machines Melikar had mentioned to her and Cam.

Before darkness had fallen, she'd spotted flying animals, too. Mandria had plenty of bats, mostly a bother, but these were cute and feathery, perched along fences and in trees or flitting alongside the same route they followed.

Adam stepped into the aisle and leaned against the seat, facing her. His fair hair was much shorter than Cam's. His blue-green eyes matched Mondo's, only they were not as intense.

The lad's curious gaze made Quinn fidget. Why did his nearness cause her heartbeat to lift the way it did when she raced with her childmates through the outer tunnels?

He wrinkled his brow as if he were trying to solve a puzzle. "Where are you from?" he asked.

"Mandria."

"I thought that was your last name."

Were people here not identified by their homeland?

Adam tilted his head, looking skeptical. "Is Mandria a suburb?"

She nodded, pretending to understand.

"So where are you going?" he asked.

"Um, to the kingdom." She gave a vague wave toward the window, wishing she knew what the kingdom was called.

"Kingdom," Adam repeated. "Still playing the role of a princess, are you? We peasants prefer to call it the city."

Quinn glanced at him. Adam certainly didn't look as tattered and thin as a Mandrian peasant boy.

"Why didn't you change out of your costume?" He pointed at her gown. "You're bound to attract attention dressed like that." Not waiting for an answer, he gave her another perplexed look and returned to his seat.

Attract attention. That's exactly what the princess did *not* want. She knew she stood out in her Mandrian gown, but what was she supposed to do? Glancing at other travelers, she realized how many of them were staring while trying not to.

She'd have to find proper clothes to wear while in this world, but how could she barter for them? She had nothing of value—except Cam's ring—and it might appear worthless to merchants here.

Feeling self-conscious, the princess tried to fold her billowy skirts so they were not so noticeable. Her appearance was disgraceful: her gown, torn and dusty; her hair falling loose from its braid after her dash through what Sarah had called WonderLand Park.

She thought of her mother. The queen would be mortified by her daughter's tattered appearance. She would chastise the princess's ladies for not properly attending to her daughter. Cydlin would be distraught over the reprimand. Gwynell would giggle behind cupped hands after the queen turned away.

And what would happen tonight at the evening feast when the princess's chair remained empty? Quinn's heart lurched just considering it. She hoped Gwynell would keep her wits about her. The lass was only nine-years-old and easily gave in to hysteria. Cydlin was the same age as the princess and more self-composed. She would never let on to the queen that anything was wrong. The two ladies had covered for her before when she'd lost track of time and did not arrive at the royal tower when expected.

The darker the night became, the more ill at ease the princess felt. *I am traveling far from the wishing pool—and home—with no idea where I'm going. How will I ever find my way back to Mandria?*

She always assumed any adventure above the pool would take place near the footbridge, giving her the option of returning through the portal between worlds whenever she pleased. *Why was I so drawn to follow the Dover family?*

The uneasiness soared into panic. It was almost feast time. *Where will I stay the night? Why didn't Cam give me fair warning?*

If they'd planned this venture in advance, she would have brought a change of gowns, one of her ladies, and gold pieces for food and lodging at an inn.

Mondo had seemed friendly, but how could she tell him she needed assistance? He was a stranger. Could she trust him?

As if he'd read her mind, Mondo turned to speak to her. "In a few minutes, we'll be stopping at our car. Come with us, Quinn. You will be our guest while you're visiting the city." He touched two fingers to his right cheek, tracing the line of a backward seven.

"What?" said Sarah. "She's not visiting the city. She's just going home on the shuttle." Sarah faced her. "Aren't you?"

Quinn didn't answer. Her gaze remained fixed on the old man.

He'd given her the Sign of the Lorik! An ancient Mandrian sign of trust and secrecy. Those who shared the sign shared a bond that could not be broken. It was one of the highest Mandrian truths.

Quinn now knew what she'd already sensed. She could trust Mondo completely. Her hand trembled as she lifted it to her cheek to return the Lorik sign.

Mondo continued as if nothing unusual had transpired between them. "Sarah will lend you some of her clothes."

"What?" Sarah said again, making a "tsking" sound as though offended at not being consulted. She gave Quinn a sidelong frown. "Do you go to Caprock High? I've never seen you there, and I'm sure I'd remember someone with hair as long as yours."

"Um, no," Quinn stammered. *Caprock High? What is that?* "I truly am here on a visit."

She hoped her words sounded convincing. Everything was happening too fast. She'd meant to come to this world *only* as an observer. Her mind blurred with visions of staying with this family and wearing Sarah's clothes.

"Wait a minute." Adam leaned over the seat, looking puzzled. "Your parents let you visit the city alone? And you're traveling without luggage or regular clothes?" He glanced suspiciously from his grandfather to Quinn. "What's going on? This doesn't make sense."

"Are you a runaway?" Sarah asked. "Are you hiding from the law?"

The law? Why is she wishing the worst for me?

"Enough, you two," Mondo ordered. "Be patient. When we get home Quinn will tell you who she really is and will answer all of your questions."

"Pardon?" She felt faint. "But I can't . . . how did you—?"

Before she could put her shock into words, the dragon—or "shuttle," as Sarah had called it—pitched forward and stopped.

Quinn peered out the window. They were in a field full of carriages. Sarah nudged her out of the seat and into queue with the other travelers as they made their way to the exit.

Outside, Adam and Sarah climbed into one of the small carriages. Mondo pulled Quinn aside. "My child," he whispered, "I know of Mandria. You must give me your complete trust."

He placed a hand on her shoulder, then quickly withdrew it.

So. He knew the rules of royal protocol.

"It's imperative that you stay with us while you're in this world," Mondo added. "Our meeting at the wishing pool was not by chance."

How could he know of my arrival? Quinn wondered. *Melikar? Did the wizard hold power in both worlds?*

Mondo hurried on before she could respond. "I don't have time to answer questions now, but you must tell Adam and Sarah the truth. I give you my solemn pledge your secret will be safe with them." Again he touched two fingers to his cheek.

Uncertainty tightened Quinn's throat. How could she return the sign? Not when he was asking her to break her vow to the wizard. How could she possibly reveal the secret of her kingdom?

"Melikar has spoken," the old man whispered.

Hearing the wizard's name caught her off guard. Yet, those were precisely the words she needed to hear in order to trust this man.

With a shaking hand, the princess returned the sign.

6

Telling the Secret

Mondo steered the carriage a short distance, stopping in front of a row of identical cottages, one piled on top of the other.

"Go inside and make Quinn feel welcome while I'm at work," he said.

The instant the three climbed from the carriage, Adam and Sarah began to rain a multitude of questions upon the princess.

Weary from the excitement and turmoil of her journey, Quinn raised both palms to stop them. "Can we not go inside your cottage first?"

"Cottage?" Sarah repeated. "You mean, apartment."

The princess did not like the way the maiden made her feel foolish each time she spoke. Perhaps after everything was explained, Sarah would be more understanding.

They climbed a flight of stairs. Sarah unlocked the door to one of the matching "apartments" with a key hanging from a ribbon around her neck.

The instant they stepped through the doorway, light filled the chamber. Quinn did not know how candles could be lit so quickly. Glancing around, she did not even *see* any candles, yet light filled the entire room—even the corners where a candle's glow usually failed to reach.

They led her into a large chamber and offered her a seat on a bench padded with stuffed cushions. Furnishings below the river were mostly made of wood, but this room was filled with many types of materials and colors—rugs, cabinets, chairs, and small tables. The room felt cozy. She tried to take it all in before beginning "the talk," according to Mondo's instructions.

"Quit stalling," Sarah insisted, sitting on the cushioned bench next to Quinn, "and tell us who you really are."

Adam, who possessed more patience than his sister, passed around the bread and meat Mondo had purchased during the journey home.

Quinn took hungry bites of her evening feast, despite the worried knot in her stomach. There was no getting around it. She had to trust Mondo's judgment and tell Adam and Sarah the truth.

Please do not let me endanger the secret of my kingdom, she prayed to the High Spirit.

Setting aside the food, the princess straightened, trying to look as regal as she could under the circumstances. "I am Princess Quinn from the Kingdom of Mandria."

The silence of their disbelief drifted across the room. Were they waiting for her to laugh and say she was merely jesting?

"You mean you're a *real* princess?" Sarah asked in a voice overflowing with skepticism.

Quinn nodded, fidgeting with her braid because the two were making her nervous with their stares.

"So, where is your kingdom?" Adam asked.

Unsure how to respond, she simply said, "Beneath the river."

Doubt clouded his eyes. "What river?"

"Beneath the Mandrian River. Where the wishing pool is."

Sarah's eyes lit up at the mention of the pool. "Oh, the wishing pool. I love it there; it's so peaceful."

"That's not the Mandrian River," Adam said. "It's the Canadian River. At least, that's what we call it."

Sarah hugged her knees to her chest. "I go right to the wishing pool whenever Mondo takes us to Wonder-Land Park."

"I know," Quinn said. "Once, you wished to be beautiful."

The maiden gasped, shooting an embarrassed glance at her brother. "How did you know that?"

"I've seen you—and heard you—from beneath the pool."

Silence.

Adam shifted away, as if wanting to distance himself from this peculiar conversation. "What exactly do you mean by 'beneath the pool'?" he asked.

All Quinn could do was answer honestly, even if the whole idea of another world existing so close to theirs seemed bizarre. "Directly beneath the pool lies the wizard's chamber in the uppermost tower of my father's castle," she explained. "The castle sits in the heart of Mandria, the largest of the underground kingdoms."

The princess did not like feeling as though they believed she was inventing a faery tale when, in fact, she was telling the absolute truth. Holding the lad's gaze, she silently implored him to believe her story.

Adam shoved away his feast. "This is too weird."

"Weird is right," Sarah added, scooting to the opposite end of the padded bench—away from the princess.

Quinn doubted the two would believe the rest of her story, but she'd promised Mondo. Taking a deep breath, she told them about her life in the other world, describing the castle, the Marnies, Melikar.

They listened intently, as though she were telling a childhood fable.

"Now it's your turn," she finished, eager to change the subject and learn more about their world. "Tell me about Mondo."

Adam shook his head, as if re-directing his thoughts to the present. "What's to tell?" he said. "He's our grandfather."

"How does he know of Mandria?"

Adam looked at his sister and shrugged.

"We don't know," Sarah said. "He's never mentioned

it to us."

"But we haven't known him very long," her brother added. "Mondo came here after our parents died in a car accident two years ago. He was our only living relative, so he became our legal guardian."

Quinn had wondered about their parents but felt it wasn't proper to ask.

"Our mother used to mention Mondo," Sarah said. "But she never knew where he was, except when he sent a card or called." The maiden's voice trembled when she mentioned her mother. "Our grandmother died before we were born, and afterward, it was too hard for Mondo to stay in the home they'd shared, so he started moving here and there."

"We don't know how he heard about our parents' accident," Adam said, "but he came for us right away, hired on as a cabinetmaker for a local furniture company, and moved us into this apartment."

Quinn's heart went out to them over the sadness they'd endured. Still, she wondered about Mondo's connection to Mandria.

Sarah began to chuckle. "Wait till the kids at school hear—"

"No!" The princess's earlier feeling of panic gripped her once more. "Mondo promised you'd keep my secret."

Sarah made a face, looking disappointed.

Adam reached to nudge his sister. "You can't tell anyone, Sis. Who would believe you, anyway?"

She shrugged.

"It might put Quinn in danger if anyone found out," he added. "Promise you won't tell?"

Sarah nudged him back. "You're taking all the fun out of it."

"Your brother is right," Quinn told her. "You must keep this an absolute secret." She taught them the Sign of the Lorik and explained what it meant. "It's a Mandrian truth," she whispered.

"You don't have to whisper," Sarah said, looking peeved at not being allowed to talk about the other-world princess who'd come to visit.

"I don't want the servants to hear," Quinn said.

Adam and Sarah looked at each other and laughed.

"Servants?" Adam repeated. "I don't think so. There must be lots of differences between our worlds. Maybe you'll need a private tutor while you're here." He stood and bowed with a flourish. "Allow me to instruct you, oh beautiful princess."

Quinn felt herself blushing. Did he truly think she was beautiful? *She'd* never thought so. Her nose had been crooked from the time Scrabit darted in front of Trinka, sending her tumbling from the pony's saddle. And her eyelashes were so pale they could barely be seen.

Quinn glanced at the magic ring on her finger. Could she wish for beauty? Like Sarah? The memory of Melikar's disgust over trivial wishes was her answer. "*Magic is mighty,*" he'd said. "*And must be used for mighty purposes.*"

Sarah acted annoyed by her brother's attentiveness

toward the princess. "So, are you going to school with us tomorrow?"

"School? I–I don't know." The idea had not occurred to Quinn, yet it was intriguing.

"I think you should," Adam told her. "I mean, if you want to get an idea of what life is like in our world, you should experience a few days at a high school. You won't learn much by staying here in the apartment."

The lad's suggestion seemed important. She thought of Cam. He'd want her to have a jolly time—to get a real taste of life in this world. And if young folk went to what Adam called "high school," then perhaps she should tag along.

"Very well," she told them. "I shall go."

Sarah nodded as if she agreed. "I'd better lay out clothes for you, because you can't show up at Caprock High wearing a medieval gown."

Quinn did not know what "medieval" meant, but she got the maiden's point.

Sarah rose, grabbing her untouched feast. "I guess you'll have to sleep in my room. There's an extra bed in there for *invited* guests."

The princess did not miss the sarcasm. Why was Sarah so contrary? All the maidens in Mandria were at Quinn's beck and call. No one ever talked back, much less insulted her.

Quinn bit her lip, resisting the urge to lecture the maiden on proper behavior in the presence of royalty. But why should she care if Sarah liked her? The kingdom of Mandria would continue to exist whether or not this foolish maiden believed in it.

The princess watched Sarah disappear down a corridor in the apartment. She'd best keep peace, especially if she had to depend on the maiden while attending lessons with her.

Adam sprawled on the floor, studying Quinn with such intensity it made her nervous. Suddenly a kitten with white fur tore through the chamber and sprang onto Quinn's lap, startling her.

She reached a timid hand to pet him. Marnies were the sole keepers of cats, so they were rare in upper Mandria. The Marnie tunnels often swarmed with the creatures the same size as this tiny one.

Adam chuckled at her reaction. "This is our new kitten. My German teacher gave him to us, so we named him *Katze*. It's German for 'cat.'"

"German?" Quinn felt more comfortable asking Adam questions. He did not make her feel foolish the way Sarah did.

"Um." He paused to raise an eyebrow. "The language spoken in the country of Germany?"

"Oh." The knowledge that everyone in this world did not speak the same language surprised her.

"Wow," he said. "I think being your tutor will keep me busy."

Quinn laughed at the goofy face he made. She relaxed against the cushions for the first time since she'd sat down. The tension cramping her neck had disappeared the moment Sarah left the room. Why did Adam accept her, yet his sister refused?

He grabbed the kitten off Quinn's lap and wrestled with him on the floor. "Tell me about school in Mandria."

"I do not go to school."

"Why not?"

"Because there I really *do* have a tutor. Her name is Ameka."

Adam looked impressed.

"I *am* a princess," she reminded him.

"How could I forget?" he teased. "Look at you." The lad cocked his head. "If you don't go to school, then you probably don't go to parties."

"Oh, we have many balls at the castle."

"Do you dance?"

"Of course. It's part of a princess's instruction on being a lady."

"Whoa, that sounds pretty weird in this day and age." Adam patted Katze away and joined Quinn on the cushioned bench. "Who do you dance with at the balls?"

"Dagon, mostly, but I'm required to dance with sons of visiting dignitaries. And, if it weren't for me, Cam would not know how to dance at all."

"Are they your boyfriends?"

"My what?"

"Your . . . um, what would you call them? Your admirers? Your suitors?"

Adam's questions made her uneasy. "No. Dagon is my cousin, and Cam is the wizard's apprentice. Cam does not come from nobility, so he cannot be a proper suitor."

"A proper suitor," Adam repeated.

Her face grew warm. "Why are you asking all these questions?"

"I want to warn you—" He paused, as though choosing his words with care. "The minute you step into school tomorrow, a million guys are going to fall at your feet."

She felt flattered and alarmed at the same time. "Why would they bow before me? They will not know I'm royalty—unless you tell them, and you promised you would not."

Adam started to laugh, then stifled his reaction, as if worried he might hurt her feelings. "Let me rephrase that. You will attract a lot of attention from the boys."

"Why?" The kitten sprang back into her lap and began to purr. Quinn wondered why she'd always feared these harmless creatures. Perhaps the fear was triggered by being surrounded by a multitude of them in a Marnie tunnel.

"You'll attract attention because you're different," Adam said. "You look different, you talk differently, your skin is so incredibly pale, it's like a . . . a sheet of paper. And your hair." He took hold of her braid, pulling it in front of her shoulder. "Your hair is fantastic. No girl at school has hair this long."

Adam dropped her braid, averting his eyes. "Sorry.

Guess I got carried away."

He fell silent for a moment, turning back to gaze at her.

Quinn loved looking into his eyes. It made her dizzy.

"I guess what I'm trying to say is—" Shoving off from the bench, he paced across the chamber and back. "Will you go to the Halloween dance with me this weekend? If I don't ask you right now, someone else will beat me to it."

Quinn's heart fluttered. Adam was asking to court her!

In Mandria, it was improper to court a princess without obtaining the king's permission—a task certain to scare off even the most serious suitor. But this wasn't Mandria, so all Quinn had to answer was . . .

"Yes."

Immediately, worry struck her. What if there were rules for courting, like at home? Rules she did not know. Surely Adam would instruct her.

"Great!" was all he said, sitting beside her again.

"May I ask a question?" she began.

"Certainly."

"What is Halloween?"

Adam grinned instead of answering. "Good thing you have a tutor nearby—but I predict you'll find out for yourself in a couple of days."

A couple of days.

It sounded like a long time to be away from home. Was it wise? Melikar and Cam were probably beside themselves with worry. Her thoughts flew to her parents, making her heart stall. Surely Melikar knew how to keep them calm—didn't he?

Oh, bother.

Her head whirled with multiple details she needed to remember. It was very much like Ameka drilling her on Mandrian history with all its important dates and battles. She was expected to keep them straight and discuss them in detail with pen and parchment.

Plus, she was getting drowsy. *Perhaps I shall stay one night and one day. I shall go to lessons and have lots of amazing stories to tell Cam.*

The princess imagined the apprentice staring at her with rapt attention as she told him how it felt to wake up on the footbridge, see the prison's torture area, and travel home with this family.

After that, I shall be ready to return to Mandria.

Adam's nearness made her feel even dizzier. He stroked her cheek with the back of his hand. Though not used to being touched, she welcomed his gentle caress and the warmth . . . it cascaded through her.

The princess met his gaze. Would it be proper to ask Adam to hug her the way she'd watched couples on the footbridge hug? Was it unprincesslike to request such a thing? Adam would be the perfect one to show her.

He was so close, she could sense his heartbeat. Part of her wanted the moment to last forever, and part of her wished she were in Sarah's sleeping chamber in bed.

Tingles skittered down her spine. The room pitched

into darkness. Galloping ponies stampeded through her head, then stillness claimed her.

Coming out of a fog, the princess gingerly opened her eyes. Sarah loomed above her, eyes wide, mouth gaping.

Running footsteps sounded nearby. "Sarah!" Adam shouted. "She disappeared!" He burst through the door. "She disa—!" The sight of Quinn stopped him. "What *happened?*"

Shaken, the princess sat up. She was in Sarah's sleeping chamber in bed.

Lifting a trembling hand, she showed them Cam's ring. "I guess the magic works in both worlds. I'd better be careful what I wish."

The flicker of doubt she'd seen earlier in Sarah's eyes was gone. In one instant display of magic, she'd earned Sarah's belief—as well as Adam's, had he any misgivings.

"What *else* can you do with the ring?" Sarah asked, flopping onto the foot of the bed. "Show us more magic!"

The princess untangled her braid from the coverlet. "I cannot."

"Why?" they both asked.

"Because our wizard—Melikar—allows no one to use magic lightly—especially for amusement. It's a Mandrian truth."

Sarah frowned. "Qui–inn, that's ridiculous. Come on, do something else."

The princess lay back, yanking a quilt over her head. Why all this fuss over a little magic? If they'd seen *half* the enchantments she'd witnessed in Mandria—

Sarah jerked away the quilt. "The wizard is not here," she persisted. "And—"

A tinkling melody interrupted Sarah's plea, making Quinn's heart leap. What was *that*? A sign from the wizard, telling her he *was* here? Hovering invisibly in this world? Keeping an eye on her to make sure she upheld all Mandrian truths?

Adam reached for something silver on the dresser and held it to his ear. He said a few words, then set the object down in some sort of holder. "That was Mondo. He wanted to make sure everything was all right."

Now it was Quinn's turn to be stunned. "But I thought magic was gone from this world."

They laughed instead of answering.

Adam gave a tired sigh. "I think I have a full day of tutoring ahead, so I'll say good-night. My brain's had all it can handle of underground kingdoms and disappearing princesses."

After he left, Sarah climbed into the other bed without saying any more.

Quinn climbed out of bed. She'd never prepared for sleep by herself. Her ladies always turned down the quilt, warmed the bed with hot stones from the fire, then helped her undress and unbraid her hair.

Removing the gown by herself was not easy with all the tiny buttons lining the back from neck to hips. After a frustrating few minutes, she accomplished the tedious task, then draped the dress over a chair. Feeling modest about disrobing in front of Sarah, she reached for a sleeping garment the maiden had set out for her. Quinn slipped it on and then kicked off her jeweled Mandrian slippers.

Not bothering to unbraid her hair, the princess returned to bed as the light mysteriously blinked out. She missed her nightly goblet of candleberry tea, but was not about to ask Sarah to prepare the warm concoction for her.

In the haze before sleep, Quinn wondered why the magic ring had worked when she had not twisted it three times. Maybe its enchantment was more powerful than Cam knew.

Her thoughts turned to Melikar. Had he cast a spell from below the river to make sure she met the Dover family? Mondo had said their meeting was not by chance. Conflicting feelings of comfort and uneasiness nudged her at the thought of Melikar tracking her sojourn on Outer Earth.

Did he know she possessed the ring and had used its power—by accident? Would it anger him?

Closing her eyes in sleep, she vowed once more:

I'd better be careful what I wish.

She hoped her good intentions reached the world below.

7

This World's Magic

~

Light from the sun glistened through the window, waking the princess. Stretching, she marveled at the oddity of being awakened by daylight.

Her thoughts drifted to Mandria. What would she be doing if she were home right now?

Cydlin and Gwynell would enter her chamber to light the morning candles. They'd fill her bath with heated water from one of the underground springs in the grotto, lay out a fresh gown, and bring her a goblet of ginger tea.

The maidens would help the princess dress and would braid her hair—with Cydlin working swiftly and silently and Gwynell entertaining the princess with her foolishness. Quinn always tried not to react to the lass's antics, even though they amused and annoyed her at the same time.

The princess would join her parents in the royal tower for the morning feast. Afterward, they'd go their separate ways: the king to advisory sessions with Lord Blakely and the royal knights of counsel; the queen to meet with noble ladies of the court to plan cultural events; and Quinn to Ameka, her private tutor.

Ameka was eighteen, and though strict about Quinn minding her lessons, every once in a while she would let the princess spend an afternoon visiting an unexplored corner of the kingdom or join Cam and Dagon for a four-some of mallet and ball in the queen's garden.

Once, the group trekked off to the Marnie village to learn about woodcarving from Grizzle, an old Marnie whose patience as a lesson master did not stretch very far. Still, he allowed them to observe the carving of a wooden cabinet for Quinn's chamber.

A horrid buzzing noise exploded into her dream, shattering the pleasant images.

Sarah stirred, reaching toward a box near her bed. The buzzing stopped.

"Time to get up," she said, yawning. "You take a shower while I fix breakfast."

"Take a what?" Quinn asked.

Groaning, Sarah staggered out of bed and pulled on a gray robe. "Come on. I'll show you what a shower is." She paused. "You *do* know what breakfast is, don't you?" She smiled to show she was jesting.

Quinn smiled back, glad to see the maiden in a

nicer mood this morning.

Padding barefoot from the chamber, the princess followed Sarah across the corridor into a small room that contained a bath and a looking-glass.

The maiden offered to unbraid Quinn's hair. The princess was pleased with the assistance, even though Sarah kept marveling over the length. Did maidens in this world never grow their hair long?

Fetching a towel and soap, Sarah turned on what she called a shower. The sight of water spraying from a wall astonished the princess. "Magic!" she exclaimed.

"Plumbing," Sarah answered. "Pretend it's rain."

"Rain?"

Sarah's roll of the eyes reminded Quinn of impatient Grizzle. "You mean, you don't even know what rain is?"

"Ay, yes, I've heard Melikar complain about rain in the outer world when drops of water riddle the wishing pool and disrupt his clear-pool spell."

Sarah pulled her robe tight. "Having you around will take some getting used to." She stepped from the room and closed the door.

Quinn's first shower—with her choice of scented soaps—was invigorating, but shampooing the many handfuls of her hair without the assistance of her ladies was not easy. Doing things herself made her grateful for Cydlin and Gwynell. *Perhaps I'll surprise them with thank-you gifts from this world.* She thought they'd be especially delighted with the egg-shaped soap that smelled like gardenias.

The princess dressed in garments Sarah lent her, feeling strange in leggings made from a faded blue material. Only lads wore leggings in Mandria. The upper garment was deep scarlet, like buckthorn berries, form-fitting, and buttonless.

She was used to wearing many layers to ward off the cool dampness of the underground world, so this skimpy single layer made her wish she'd brought a traveling cape to cover herself.

Sarah had forgotten to set out shoes, so the princess stepped into her jeweled Mandrian slippers, glad to have something from home with her on this vexing day.

Untangling her damp hair, she attempted to braid it. After a frustrating few minutes, she gave up, letting it fall in waves to the back of her knees. Not having her hair plaited today was the least of her worries.

Finding her way to the kitchen, she enjoyed a morning feast of eggs, toasted bread with bits of fruit, and juice. Finally, a similarity between the two worlds.

Adam and Sarah were quiet this morning, although Adam kept staring at her. Mondo had worked late and was still asleep.

Quinn's apprehension over going to lessons with Sarah began to mount as the others prepared to leave. *Perhaps I should remain in the apartment.*

And miss the opportunity to experience a new world? her mind argued.

But I feel safe here.

You'll never get another chance.

Quinn hated it when her conscience reminded her that nothing new and different ever happened to her in Mandria.

Do it for Cam, if not for yourself, her conscience added. Yes, Cam would be so disappointed if she returned without bringing back tales of an exciting quest with which to entertain him.

She watched Adam and Sarah rush about, packing books into knapsacks. Sarah stopped in front of a looking-glass near the door to fluff her hair and smooth her garments. Adam did the same, although Quinn thought he already looked perfect.

With Cam on her mind for strength, the princess followed the Dovers outside and down the steps, shading her eyes from the morning brightness. A great yellow carriage hunched on the avenue in front of the apartments.

"It's called a school bus," Adam whispered as they boarded.

Quinn was grateful to know the proper words so she did not say the wrong thing.

Adam greeted friends, then moved to a seat in the back. Quinn sat next to Sarah and tried not to stare at young folk around her, although *they* were staring at her.

Sarah introduced her as Quinn Mandria, the Dovers' cousin. Mondo had left a note for Sarah to give to the headmaster, saying Quinn's records were coming from a previous school. He felt it would allow her a couple days' taste of lessons with few questions asked.

The plan worried Quinn, though. She hoped it did

not draw unwanted attention to her. *I plan to stay for only one day,* she reminded herself.

The princess fidgeted in her seat as the bus lumbered along a wide avenue. The borrowed clothes were uncomfortable—tight, and more revealing than her garments at home. Damp hair kept falling across her face—which actually was a blessing since it helped to shade her eyes from the morning brightness.

Trying to look like a maiden of this world was certainly not giving her the confidence she desired right now. Why was everyone gaping at her? Was it her hair? Should she cut it short like Sarah's? But then folk in Mandria would stare when she returned.

She glanced at Sarah, who looked striking in a violet garment that set off her pale hair. Purple trinkets dangled from her ears. Even her eyelids were violet. Quinn liked the way it looked and wondered how Sarah had done it.

"Quinn!" Sarah whisper-hissed. "You have on the wrong shoes."

"Mine were the only ones I could find."

Sarah squinted her eyes, as if remembering that she'd forgotten to set out shoes for the Dover's house guest. "Well, be prepared to answer if kids ask where you got them."

"What should I say?"

"Um, say you got them at the mall."

Closing her eyes, the princess memorized the new word. There was so much to remember. Silently, she asked the High Spirit to help her refrain from saying something doltish or doing anything suspicious.

A wave of anxiety rolled over her as the school bus barreled on toward the unknown. *I am ridiculously unprepared to be in this world alone.*

Apprehension mingled with homesickness as worries about her parents came to mind. Quinn knew they must be frantic by now. She had not meant to upset them.

Taking hold of the magic ring, Quinn twisted it three times. She wished Melikar might cast a spell to keep the king and queen from fretting. Would the ring's magic reach all the way to Mandria?

Rising trepidation made it hard to breathe. Quinn yanked at the neck of her garment, wishing it weren't so close-fitting.

This isn't what I wanted. Not what Cam and I planned. I do not want to be on this moving contraption, pretending to be somebody's cousin—somebody who does not even like me.

Whatever had possessed her to attend lessons at all?

I should have stayed near the wishing pool and listened to the dryads' stories. I'd rather be home, wearing my own clothes, reading for Ameka, pestering Melikar, playing with Scrabit, or arguing with Cam.

She *missed* arguing with Cam.

Imagining this world from below the river seemed a lot safer than being here.

I have to get off this machine.

Grabbing Sarah's arm, the princess leaned close to whisper. "This is not a good plan for me. I've decided to return home."

Disappointment reflected in Sarah's eyes, yet the princess wondered if it stemmed more from losing the attention her unusual "cousin" was bringing than from her actual departure.

"You can't leave now," Sarah whispered back. "I'll bet you're just homesick. I was, too, when my parents died, and we had to move out of our house."

Quinn was only half-listening. The wishing pool was the only doorway to the other world. Could she find her way back to it? Why had she not paid more attention on the trip from WonderLand Park?

"Sarah, you do not understand. I cannot—"

Giving a tiny squeal, Sarah shushed her. "Here he comes!" she whispered. "Oh, he's looking right at us. Act natural."

A tall, brawny lad with dark hair and eyes had boarded the bus and was sauntering down the aisle. On his garment was a large numeral.

Sarah giggled. "Hi, Zack," she singsonged.

The lad stopped at their seat. "Hey, Sarah," he answered. "Who's this?" Taking hold of Quinn's chin, he jerked her face upward so he could get a better look at her. Voices around them quieted as everyone watched.

Bristling, Quinn tried to pull away, but he tightened his grip. No one in Mandria would dare such an action. He'd be banished from the kingdom—or worse.

The princess glared at the insolent lad and wished he would let go.

A spark crackled between them.

Zack jerked his hand away, as if stung by a scorpion. It happened too fast for anyone but them to notice.

"What the—?" Rubbing his hand against his shirt, Zack peered more closely at her. "Who *are* you?"

"She's my cousin," explained Sarah. "Hey, you were awesome at Friday's game."

The princess was thankful for Sarah's attempt to distract the lad, but his eyes never left Quinn's face. Inside, she felt herself grow as small as a Marnie cat's mouse. *How could I be so foolish? Using magic on a stranger?*

Granted, it was an accident—and he deserved it.

Quinn averted her eyes, hoping if she ignored him he'd leave. A coldness emanated from him, chilling her heart, a coldness she hadn't felt since she'd toured the deepest dungeons of Mandria.

Disregarding Sarah, Zack leaned close to the princess and whispered, "I'll see *you* later, little cousin." His breath smelled like the spirits brewed by dwarfs in the Kingdom of Bromlia.

The lad started to touch her hair, then hesitated. Pulling his hand away, he slid into the nearest seat.

Revulsion rolled over Quinn, making her ill.

Beside her, Sarah slumped in her seat, grinning and nudging Quinn. "I think he's *so* hot, don't you?"

The princess did not have an answer to why the bothersome knave might be overheated. And, certainly, she did not care.

8

The Apprentice's Nightmare

~

Beneath the river, Cam woke in a heart-racing state from a worrisome dream. The fire on the hearth had died to a faint glow. Good thing the wizard was up and gone already, or Cam knew he'd receive a scolding for being lazy.

Rising from his cot, he shivered in the damp air as he grabbed an unlit candle from a sconce on the wall and held it close to the glowing embers until the wick burst into flame.

Shaking his head to hasten wakefulness, he wondered if his dream was merely a nightmare—or a forewarning. Most dreams—to a wizard—were premonitions, yet being a lowly apprentice, his were few and far between.

He *had* foretold the arrival of Dagon and Lord Ryswick from Pendrog Manor in Twickingham, but

Quinn insisted she'd mentioned the upcoming visit from her relatives, which planted the image in Cam's mind and triggered the dream.

Cam remembered the ensuing quarrel over whether he would ever become a master wizard like Melikar or if his powers would always be limited, due to his unknown heritage.

The apprentice stared at the wall, replaying the long-ago scene in his mind until dripping wax burned his fingers. *Bats!* he cursed, then cursed again. He *missed* arguing with the princess.

As for the question of his unknown heritage, he wished it would flee into the night like a robber and leave him be.

Cam raised the candle to the hourglass on top of the herb cabinet. Twelve hours of sand had flowed through the narrow passage, marking night's end. True, he had overslept. The bothersome dream would not allow him to awaken until it had played itself out. Or so it seemed.

Turning the glass bulb upside-down, Cam wondered how much time had passed. Unsure, he jiggled the contraption to hurry ahead the sand, hoping to make up for the missed time.

Moving about the chamber, he lit candles and rebuilt the fire. The wizard had departed at an early hour to visit the castle kitchen with the intent to secretly add doleran seeds to the royal tea that Marged, the head cook, would be preparing for the king and queen. If the unexpected visit from the wizard alarmed

Marged, or caused suspicion, Melikar held the power to make the cook forget his task once he departed.

As for last night's feast, Quinn's quick-thinking ladies concocted an excuse for her absence that, thankfully, no one questioned.

Cam set the candle in a spiked holder on the workbench, then halfheartedly reached for a broom to sweep up the latest coins rained from above. He wondered if he should gather the useless coins in a basket and cast the spell he'd cast upon Quinn, sending the basket into the other world. Surely the princess needed something of earthly value to barter for food and a place to lodge.

Quinn.

Cam could hardly bear to think about the princess. He recalled his last glimpse of her, waving good-bye from the footbridge above the wishing pool.

After Melikar had cast the spell allowing her to return, he felt as if a load of firewood had been lifted from his shoulders.

But then, nothing happened.

Knowing Quinn, she would choose to remain in the outer world. For a time, at least. But what if now she desired to come home?

Thanks to him, she did not know how.

Cam missed her terribly and had lain on his cot, wishing as many times as there were grains of sand in the hourglass that he'd spell-traveled with her.

Was she safe? Where had she stayed the night? Had she acquired food? Was she angry at him for sending her there? Or pleased with him for causing it?

Too many painful question bothered his mind, making his heart catch in his throat. Was she missing him, too?

Dropping to one knee, he swept beneath a cabinet. The broom knocked against something. The ring! This was one place he'd forgotten to look. Thrusting his arm beneath the cabinet, he searched each corner—and pulled out the ladle, which had gone flying as he'd raced to the circle of light to join the princess.

The ring wasn't there. It wasn't anywhere he'd looked. Did Quinn somehow have it? Was it possible?

Cam set the broom by the hearth and returned to his cot. He was glad for Melikar's absence because he did not feel like doing chores. Lying down, he closed his eyes to worry over the nightmare that had troubled his sleep.

In his dream, the princess was in danger. She was running through a forest. Tree branches reached out to her. Were they trying to harm or help her? He could not tell.

A young knave was chasing her. He *did* mean the princess harm—Cam could feel it. He was tall and strapping with dark hair and strange clothes. On the front of his tunic was a large numeral.

Cam wanted desperately to help the princess, but there was nothing he could do from beneath the river. As he dozed, pondering the dream, the nightmare began to unfold once more.

A knock at the portal brought him awake and to his feet. Shaking the dream from his mind, he hurried to open the door.

Ameka greeted him with a smile. "Morning, Cam." Her skirts swished past him as she stepped into Melikar's chamber. Her simply styled, moss-green dress set off her eyes of the same hue, as well as her lengths of hair the color of chestnuts.

"Quinn is late for lessons this morning. When she's tardy, I usually find her vexing Melikar." Ameka's gaze darted about the chamber as she spoke. "Is she here?"

"Ay . . . no," Cam stammered. What should he tell her? Melikar had taken care that the king and queen not discover their daughter's disappearance, but he must have forgotten the royal tutor would likewise be looking for the princess.

"Do you know where she is?" Ameka asked.

The maiden was as tall as Cam, so it was hard to avoid meeting her gaze as she faced him. "Yes," he answered, offering no more.

"Where?" Curiosity glinted in her eyes.

Cam paused. Although Melikar wanted Quinn's whereabouts kept secret, Ameka would have to be told. Touching two fingers to his cheek, he formed the Sign of the Lorik.

The sign took Ameka by surprise. "Where is she, Cam? Is she in danger?"

He answered with silence.

"So be it," she said, returning the Lorik sign. "I pledge to keep your secret." The maiden held his gaze. "Cam, this is serious. I have to answer to Queen Leah if Quinn misses a day of instruction."

"This I know," he answered, sighing. "Yet I'm not quite sure how to tell you."

"What? Is Quinn off to the Marnie village? Out for a ride on Trinka? Please tell me she hasn't left the castle grounds unattended." Concern clouded her eyes. "Oh, I hope she took Scrabit along for protection. Who knows what type of rogues might be out and about on the day before the outer world's full moon?"

Cam found it difficult to put his answer into words. "The princess is not anywhere *below* us."

Ameka gave him a puzzled look. "Well, she has to be somewhere *below* us because the only place *above* us is—"

Cam nodded, watching surprise pale Ameka's face. "She's in the other world?"

"True," he replied.

Ameka broke into excited laughter. "Jolly good! How did she—?"

Cam pointed to the wishing pool.

"The pool. Of course. The princess is forever fascinated with the other world—and now the king and queen have let her go." Ameka rushed to the circle of light beneath the pool, gazing upward. "Who escorted her?"

"No one," Cam answered in a grim voice. "And the king and queen do not know their daughter has departed from Mandria."

Ameka stared at the apprentice. Her smile faded.

Cam knew what she was thinking. No one deceived

King Marit and lived to tell about it.

"That's frightful," Ameka whispered. "I trust this explains the secrecy?"

Cam told her the details, taking full blame upon himself.

"Ay, in spite of the danger, I cannot help feeling excited for her." Ameka gazed up through the pool, turning in the circle of light for a better look.

"Stop!" Cam blurted, eyes transfixed on the water. He waited, feeling jumpy, but a whirlpool did *not* form.

Of course not, he told himself. He was getting the spell to return to Mandria mixed up with the spell to leave.

Ameka stared at him. "Cam, what is wrong?"

"Nothing." He felt foolish now. "I–I'd simply feel better if you stood still."

Ameka obeyed, craning her neck to see as much as she could of the outer world. "Oh, I do hope she writes everything down—what she sees, hears, eats. Everything she does." Stopping, she laughed at herself. "I sound like a tutor, don't I?"

Cam agreed, glancing at the now-inaccurate hourglass, hoping he was not late for his own lessons. Only royalty had the benefit of a private tutor. Melikar's influence had gotten the apprentice into classes with the sons of Mandria's nobility.

Ameka remained beneath the pool, hands clasped as though she were praying. "Is there any way you might send Quinn a message with your magic? I mean, can you give her a mental hint to keep a written record of her travels? It would be so valuable to us here when she returns."

"I'll try," Cam promised. "Indeed, I will." He chose not to mention the newest Mandrian truth: The princess did not know *how* to return.

After Ameka departed, Cam quickly finished his morning chores. He'd have to ask Melikar about conveying hints from one mind to another. When he and Quinn were younger, they played at sending each other silent messages, but it had been a long time ago.

However, he would oblige Ameka by trying. He would send hints to the princess to write of her sojourn on Outer Earth. Perhaps someday she might allow him to read the account of who was chasing her through the forest—and how the chase ended.

Fetching his knapsack, Cam threw off the foreboding feelings from the dream. Hurrying down the spiral rock steps to the castle below and the tunneled avenues beyond, he focused on another hint he planned to send the princess.

Please come home. This lowly apprentice misses you.

9

Beware of Potted Plants

~

The princess stepped off what Adam had called a school bus, lifting her gaze to take in the great stone building before her. It was the closest thing to a castle she'd seen in this world—but looked much more ominous. Still, it gave her a feeling of familiarity simply to look at the gray, rock walls.

She watched Adam exit the bus, then search the crowd until he found her. He peered at her intensely, as if watching for a sign that she really wanted to proceed with this plan of experiencing the life of a scholar in this world.

The princess nodded at him, hoping he might excuse himself from the company of his friends and escort her through the day. Instead, he cocked his head to one side in sympathy and gave her an encouraging wave before walking away with the others.

Quinn hated to see him depart. Why could she not attend classes with him instead of his acerbic sister?

"This way," Sarah said, nudging the princess toward the stone building. The maiden led her through double doors into a dimly lit corridor filled with a bustling crowd of noisy scholars. Quinn stumbled, trying to stay alongside Sarah. Absorbing all the sights, smells, and bits of conversation was difficult when she had to keep dodging young folk.

After checking in at the headmaster's chamber and leaving the note from Mondo, they continued down the corridor, stopping in front of a row of metal doors. Sarah unlocked one and opened it. In a flash, she dumped books on a shelf, grabbed others, then slammed the door, seemingly in unison with many other slamming doors the length of the hall.

The princess was curious about the metal compartment but decided to hold questions for later when Adam could answer them.

As they started down the corridor again, Quinn tried to study other maidens without gawking at them. Would she ever be able to fool anyone into thinking she was one of them? Her pale hair and skin made her feel as out of place as a faery in the Hall of the First Order of Knights.

She noticed other differences, too. Many of these maidens had lips the color of rubies in her father's crown, rosy cheeks, dark eyelashes, and shaded eyelids.

Grabbing Sarah's sleeve to slow her down, Quinn whispered, "Why do maidens wear colors on their faces?"

Sarah stopped to study Quinn's face. "Oh, *that's* what's missing. Come on." Taking Quinn's elbow, she steered her sideways through the crowd and pushed open a door marked *"GIRLS"*.

Inside the chamber, a row of doors covered one wall, and a row of washbasins ran along the other. Above the basins stretched a long looking glass. A dozen maidens vied for spots in front of their reflections, combing their hair and coloring their faces. The maidens chittered to each other, reminding Quinn of the chirpy red-feathered trega birds in the orchards beneath the river.

Sarah finagled a spot in front of the looking glass, then jerked Quinn into place. Digging into her bag, she pulled out a variety of small pots. Twisting off the tops, she dabbed the contents onto the princess's face.

It tickled. Quinn had a hard time standing still, especially when Sarah combed her eyelashes with a tiny brush.

"Voilà!" Sarah exclaimed. Grasping Quinn's shoulders, she turned the princess to face her reflection.

Toads and mugwort! Quinn thought, catching herself before expressing the Mandrian saying out loud. Her lips were as crimson as her garment, her cheeks blushed on their own, and her eyelids matched the earthen hue of a Mandrian tunnel. But the best part of all were her eyelashes. No longer pale and colorless, now they were full and long and dark—like Ameka's.

She'd always been envious of Ameka's lashes.

The princess was unsure how to react in front of Sarah, and she did not want to seem unappreciative. "Ay," she finally exclaimed. "Now I look like a court jester."

The chittering stopped as all eyes turned toward the princess.

"A court jester?" Sarah repeated. Nervously, she glanced at the other maidens, then pretended to be amused. "Oh, yes, a court jester. Like Mrs. Brill was telling us about in drama. Very funny."

The princess knew Sarah was covering up for her and attempting to help her blend in.

Sarah dumped the color pots into her bag, then shoved Quinn past the staring lasses toward the door. The princess couldn't help but grin at them. A little Outer-Earth magic, and *poof*! Gone were her pale skin and lashes.

Wait till I tell Cam. He will not understand it at all, yet he'll listen attentively, ask questions, and laugh in all the right places.

Back in the crowded hallway, the princess thought she'd feel less conspicuous, but instead, the change made her feel even more noticeable. Rushing along beside Sarah, she bowed her head, letting her hair fall across her "new" face.

"Where are we going now?" she asked, practically shouting so Sarah could hear above the noise in the corridor.

"Homeroom," Sarah called back.

"Home? But we just got here."

Sarah gave her the look that meant she'd said something foolish. "Homeroom is the first class of the day. You'll like Mr. French."

A loud bell rang, startling the princess. This world seemed to be filled with ringing bells and buzzing buzzers. Her ears longed for the quiet of the kingdom below.

Sarah disappeared through a portal with the numeral 31 above it. Quinn followed, watching scholars scramble for writing tables. The neat rows of tables and chairs reminded Quinn of the chamber where Cam took his lessons.

"Study time," the headmaster called. Had Sarah called him Master French? "Get out something to do," he ordered.

Quinn chose an empty table in the back so she could observe.

Sarah took a seat in front, then passed Quinn a writing stylus and a pile of parchment. At least it looked like parchment, but it was much thinner with faint blue lines.

Suddenly a voice boomed from a small box above the doorway. *Ay, the box traps voices, like the contrivance in Sarah's chamber that trapped Mondo's voice last night. Magic!*

The voice in the box spoke of something called a football game and a Halloween dance. Quinn did not know what type of game "football" was, but she recalled Adam's invitation to the ball called Halloween.

She relaxed into her chair to think about the Outer-Earth lad and the way he'd looked at her last night. The thought of being courted by him gave her a tingly feeling, starting at the top of her head and—

Wait. The princess jerked upright in her chair. That tingly feeling only happened when magic was present.

What was I just thinking? Did I accidentally wish for something?

Quinn felt certain she had not wished on the ring by accident.

Turning in her chair, she spotted a lone geranium in an earthen pot on the window sill. In front of the pink flower, a wisp of a wood nymph hovered like a puff of smoke.

"What is happening?" cried a tiny voice Quinn could barely hear. "Are you a witch?"

The princess felt blood drain from her face. In one instant, the entire secret of Mandria could be revealed—by a blabbering wood nymph.

"Please, hush!" Quinn whispered.

"Oh, this is wonderful!" the dryad exclaimed.

Scholars stirred, as if sensing the magic. Quinn was thankful the creature's voice was faint. The loud voice still blasted from the box above the portal. Otherwise, it would have been hard to explain.

"I can move!"

"Be quiet," Quinn pleaded. "You do not understand

what is—"

"Miss Mandria?" came a deep voice from the front of the chamber. Mr. French peered at her over the top of his spectacles. He glanced at a scroll in his hand as he moved to get a better look at his newest scholar. "Miss Quinn Mandria, is it? Please find something to do, or I will give you an assignment."

"Yes, Sire."

Scholars around her snickered. The master frowned as if he thought she was being sarcastic.

Embarrassed, Quinn hunched over the parchment, contemplating what to write. All morning, an overwhelming urge to record all that was happening to her had been tapping on her shoulder. Now was her chance.

She searched the desk for an inkwell but could not find one. Then she realized the ink came from *inside* the stylus Sarah had given her. *What a jolly good idea.*

Quinn attempted to ignore the indecipherable mumblings coming from the wood nymph and concentrate on her writing. All of a sudden, the voice from the box stopped. Quiet filled the room. Quiet, except for the enchanted geranium's gibberish. Scholars began to glance around the room, searching for the source of the voice.

"That is enough!" Quinn whispered, louder than she'd meant to.

"Miss Mandria, do I have to ask you a second time?" The schoolmaster rose from his desk, cocking an ear in her direction. "Are you playing music?"

The nymph had burst into song.

The princess grabbed her parchment and fled to an empty table as far from the flower as she could get. Sarah's disapproving frown followed her.

She thinks I'm drawing attention to myself on purpose, but nothing could be further from the truth.

Quinn ducked her head but knew everyone was watching her. How could she blend in if she could not get away from the magic?

Mr. French's shadow fell across her table. "I don't know what school you've come from, young lady, but we have rules here that are meant to be followed. If you've got an iPod or a cell phone, I suggest you leave it in your locker, or it will be confiscated."

Quinn glanced sideways at Sarah, who was now watching with sympathetic eyes. She hoped she could remember the strange words the master just spoke so she could ask the maiden later what they meant.

Sarah discretely touched two fingers to her cheek, forming the Sign of the Lorik, as if reminding Quinn of the secret they shared.

Quinn waited until Mr. French moved away, then nodded at Sarah, returning the sign.

Of course I will keep the secret of Mandria, she vowed. *It is imperative that my world remain unknown and undetected.*

10

Blending In

fter homeroom, the rest of the morning ran smoothly. No one—human nor enchanted creature—singled out the princess. She made a point not to speak to anyone—or to sit near any plants.

The lessons on world history intrigued her, since she knew so little about historical events of Outer Earth. The schoolmaster gave a lecture on Third-World countries. Quinn wondered where the first and second worlds were.

She scribbled plenty of notes. Would this be news to Melikar? Or was he knowledgeable about all three worlds?

In English literature, she read a story from a book called *King Arthur and His Knights of the Round Table*. Quinn was thrilled to find the book full of stories about her long-ago relative, King Arthur. She'd heard the sad love story of Arthur and Guinevere many times, and it always made her misty-eyed.

Her family's link to people in this world was surprising, yet understandable, since the underground kingdoms had once existed here. For generations, magic had touched the lives of underworld folk, transforming them into a race that was similar to Outer-Earth people, yet more in touch with all things supernatural.

Quinn began to relax. Melikar had nothing to worry about. She had not given away any secrets. After a shaky start, she now seemed to be fitting into this world just fine.

The last lesson before the noon feast was called algebra. The princess did not know what the word meant, but a quick glance at the textbook told her it had something to do with numerals. She was good at numerals.

The schoolmistress wrote formulas and equations on a green wall at the front of the chamber. They reminded Quinn of formulas Melikar used in his potions, albeit there was a great difference between finding the distance "from one rail station to another" and finding an antidote for the bite of a spiky grotto snake.

The *problem* with algebra was that Zack was in the class. He watched her with narrowed eyes, making her feel as out of place as a dragon in the queen's garden.

The princess thought about wishing Zack into the next kingdom, then realized she did not know if there *were* other kingdoms in this world.

After class, Sarah asked her to wait in the hall while she spoke to the mistress about her marks. As Quinn stepped into the corridor, Zack bumped into her, causing her books to spill from her hands. She sensed he'd done it on purpose.

The princess knelt to gather her books, hoping Zack would be gone when she stood. He wasn't.

"Hey, little cousin," he said. "You're going to the Halloween dance with me on Friday." Not waiting for an answer, he turned abruptly and strode away.

The icy feeling surrounding him chilled Quinn. "I cannot," she called to his retreating form.

"Yeah, you can," he threw back over one shoulder.

"No!" She ran after him, balancing the armload of books she'd collected during each class. "I already have an escort."

Zack stopped and faced her. "You already have an *escort*?" he repeated, mimicking her. "Who? Or should I say, *whom*?"

The hallway filled with other scholars, which drew attention the princess did not desire.

"I will attend the ball with Adam," Quinn said.

"Adam Dover? You're going on a date with a *relative*?"

"He's not . . . well . . . ," Quinn remembered the story Sarah had told everyone. Was being escorted by a relative taboo here? In Mandria, it was common.

She did not know what to say. Why was Zack taunting her like this? Quinn's eyes firmly met his. "I am *not* attending the ball with you." Before he could respond, she turned to hurry away—and immediately bumped into Sarah.

"There you are." Sarah's gaze traveled beyond her to Zack's retreating form. The maiden's smile disappeared. "What did he want with *you?*"

Was Sarah unhappy about the attention Zack was giving her?

Ay, so am I.

"Nothing," Quinn answered, "he was just talking." She hoisted the lesson books onto one hip, sorry that Gwynell was not here to help carry them.

How could Sarah be fond of a knave who acted the way Zack did? He did not deserve any maiden's devotion.

Sarah waved a hand as if it didn't matter. "Let's go to lunch," she said.

They climbed a stairway that led to a gigantic chamber marked "CAFETERIA." The aroma of the noon feast reminded Quinn she was hungry—a feeling she was not used to. A mere snap of her fingers in Mandria brought any delicacy she desired.

"Follow me," Sarah called above the sounds of clinking utensils and loud voices, "And do what I do."

They joined the end of a line of scholars. The princess watched Sarah select dishes of food and put them onto a tray, so she did the same. She chose a dish that looked like sauce of the apple, bread, and a baked egg. Something up ahead smelled delicious. Quinn craned her neck to see the flavorful dish. Its spicy aroma reminded her of the kitchen in the lowest level of the castle, run with an iron hand by Marged, the head cook. Quinn remembered rescuing quiet Cydlin from life as a kitchen maid after learning the lass could not abide Marged's fits of temper and thus spent most of her days in tears.

Absorbed by the process of the orderly line, the princess kept one eye on the selection with the intriguing smell. It was in a dish the size of a knight's shield, although rounder. A servant was cutting the food into slices.

"What is that?" Quinn whispered, pointing.

"Pizza," Sarah whispered back.

The princess had never seen anything like it and hoped for a taste. The aroma alone was making her mouth curious.

She watched those in the line ahead choose the dish until there were only a few slices left. *Bats*, Quinn swore, borrowing Cam's favorite curse. Sarah would receive the last piece.

Quinn scanned the area. No one was watching; there was too much commotion in the chamber. As Sarah scooped the last piece onto her plate and moved on, the princess took a deep breath, twisted the magic ring, and wished for one more slice.

Her hand was there to grab it the moment it appeared.

Warmth flushed her cheeks until the tingling sensation subsided.

She waited with dread for one of the scholars to gasp and say, "Did anyone see that?"

Moments passed. No one said a word. Pleasure made her smile as she licked spicy sauce from her fingers.

A sudden image of the wizard rose in her mind, cutting short her feeling of pleasure. She shivered as though a blast of cold wind had whooshed through the chamber. *What possessed you to use the magic?* she chided herself. *Especially on something so trivial?*

A vague premonition of danger crept up her spine. *Foolish of you to ignore Melikar's warning.*

Yes, yes. The princess agreed with the voice of her conscience, knowing she deserved the reprimand.

Sarah was bartering for her lunch with a large matron, who pushed beeping buttons on top of a slanted box. Quinn nudged Sarah. "I have nothing with which to barter."

"It's okay." Sarah told her as she handed bills and coins to the matron. "Mondo gave me lunch money for both of us."

Quinn recognized the coins. She'd seen similar ones scattered across the floor of Melikar's chamber.

As she picked up her lunch tray and stepped from the line, the princess bumped into someone. Even before turning, she knew it was Zack.

Quinn's stomach clenched so tightly she felt ill. How long had Zack been standing there? What had he seen?

"There's something weird about you," the lad whisper-growled, refusing to let her pass. "And I aim to figure it out." He faked a smile so others in the area would think they were merely chatting. "But just so you know . . . I'll be watching . . ."

The princess hurried after Sarah to an empty spot at a long table of maidens. After the thrill of obtaining the wonderful new food for her noon feast, the worry over whether or not Zack had seen the magic would certainly prevent her from enjoying it.

11
Unwanted Attention

The princess perched on a long bench, stair-stepping down to a grassy meadow stretching out below. The meadow was enclosed by an egg-shaped path. On the grass, a group of lads, including Zack, raced from one end of the giant field to the other, chasing after a ball. Quinn wondered about the ball's elongated shape. What good was a ball that would not bounce?

"Hey!" called a voice.

The princess lifted a hand to shield her eyes from the painful brightness of the sun.

Adam sprinted up the benches and sat beside her. "What are you doing out here by yourself?"

"Waiting for Sarah."

Quinn gestured toward the end of the meadow where Sarah chatted with other maidens and a lad with red hair.

"She did not want to lose me, so she brought me along, then made me stay up here while she talked to her friends."

Quinn knew she did not have to mention the obvious— that Sarah wanted to get rid of her "royal shadow"—at least for a while.

"Mmmm," Adam said. "Sarah didn't come out here to talk to friends. She came to watch *Zack*." He pronounced the lad's name as though it were a curse.

Quinn silently agreed with his reaction.

"He's a jerk," Adam said. "He's decent when he hasn't been drinking, but once he starts, his personality changes. Sarah's made a fool of herself over him for months—lightening her hair because he likes blondes, hanging around, waiting for him to notice her."

The princess loved how concerned Adam was for his sister, as if he wanted to protect her. It reminded her of the way Cam fussed whenever they ventured outside castle walls on one of their jaunts. Of course, Cam's "concern" may have been nothing more than Melikar's life-or-death warning that her safety was his sole responsibility.

Adam pulled an orange-and-white cap from his knapsack and put it on. The front stuck out like the bill of a duck, shading his face. "Caprock Longhorns" was printed along the side. "Sometimes I think my sister sent her good sense on a permanent vacation."

He glanced at the princess. "I don't like the way Zack is tailing you. It was dumb of me to think he wouldn't notice you right off."

Quinn brushed windblown hair from her face. "What makes you think he is following me?"

"I *know* he is—because I am, too." Adam grinned at her, shrugging. "But I just want to make sure you're all right."

Shoving his hands into the pockets of his jacket, he scooted close, nudging Quinn with one shoulder. "You look great in my sister's clothes. And I like your hair unbraided, too."

Quinn met his gaze. Relaxing with Adam meant she could let down her guard and say whatever she pleased, like she could with Cam. Sarah acted as though Quinn's "mistakes" were meant for her own personal embarrassment.

Adam reached for her hand. "I really like you." His words were soft compared to shouts coming from the meadow.

Quinn took a breath to calm the fluttering in her heart. *He's holding my hand!* "I like you, too," she whispered.

The noise on the field seemed far away as she focused all her attention on the lad, right here, right now.

He smoothed her hair, then traced her cheek with his fingers. "When did you start wearing makeup?"

"It was your sister's idea. She—"

Before Quinn could finish, Adam kissed her gently, slowly, sending a rush of warmth through her, chasing away autumn's chill.

Her first kiss.

She wanted the moment to last forever—but this time, she was careful not to wish it away.

Adam kissed her again. The princess sensed a spark between them that had *nothing* to do with the magic ring.

"Heads up!" a voice shouted.

A ball came hurtling toward them.

Adam leaped to his feet to catch it, while Quinn scuttled out of the way.

Zack sprinted up the benches toward them. He wore a helmet on his head and armor on his shoulders—but it was different from any knight's armor she'd ever seen.

Adam flung the ball into the burly lad's stomach.

Zack barely faltered as he caught it. He planted himself in front of Quinn and Adam, feet spread as wide as the smirk on his face. "Hey, Dover, Coach wants to see you." He tossed the ball from one hand to the other. "Right now. Pronto. Hurry up."

Adam faced Zack's glower. "I play baseball. Why would the football coach want to see me?" Offering his hand to the princess, Adam said. "Come on. Let's get out of here."

Quinn followed, hopping from one bench to the next, trying to keep her balance. She glanced back at Zack, still watching through slitted eyes as he spiraled the ball into the air. Quickly, she looked away, angry at herself for giving him her attention.

"Shouldn't we wait for Sarah?" she asked, stepping off the last bench.

Sarah was watching them with great curiosity.

Quinn waved.

Scowling, Sarah turned away.

The princess inhaled sharply, glancing at Adam to see if he'd observed Sarah's reaction.

He shrugged. "She's probably mad because Zack went up the bleachers to talk to you and didn't even speak to her." His voice still sounded tight.

"But—"

"It's okay. She'll get over it."

Adam started walking toward the school building. "We've missed the bus by now. Sarah can catch a ride with friends, and if we hurry, we can snag a lift with my buddy, Roger, before he leaves the chem lab."

As they rounded a corner, a honking sound from the avenue caught their attention.

"Need a ride?" a voice called from a faded orange carriage as it slowed to a stop.

Adam waved at the driver, then led Quinn to the avenue and opened the back door of the carriage so she could climb inside.

The lad in front turned to greet her. "Howdy. Welcome to Roger's taxi."

The princess wondered what a "taxi" was as she returned his greeting. His eyes and skin were as golden brown as folk from the kingdom of Chelwick. She'd noticed other scholars with varying shades of skin color and wondered about the connection between races above and below the earth.

Adam climbed into a seat in front. With a lurch and

a jerk, they were off, careening down the avenue.

Quinn studied the inside of the carriage, decorated with stickers, signs, and pictures—mostly of pretty girls. It was quite different from Mondo's carriage.

During the ride home, Roger and Adam talked and jested, switching topics so rapidly, Quinn felt more confused than informed.

Trying to interpret their conversation was a strain. Giving up, she watched, captivated, as Roger steered—moving levers, pushing buttons, yelling at other carriage drivers, and singing along with music coming from somewhere in front of them.

"I truly like your carriage," she told him during a lull in conversation.

Roger turned, shooting her a puzzled look.

She heard Adam groan, but he was too far away to whisper a correction to her mistake. Quinn melted into the seat as Roger attempted to peer at her through a tiny looking glass in front of him and keep his eyes on the avenue at the same time.

She bit her lip. *How am I supposed to pick my words carefully? I never know if I've said something wrong until it's too late.*

12

Unanswered
Questions

~

After Roger delivered the princess and Adam to
the Dover home and departed, Adam retreated to his
sleeping chamber to do his lessons. The princess wandered into Sarah's room and curled up on the bed. She
wanted to record the events of the past two days in a
journal Adam had given her. The book, bound in cloth
and tied with a blue ribbon, was blank inside with lines
for her to write on.

Sarah arrived, quickly gathered a few things, and left.
Why was she being so unfriendly? All because of Zack?

The princess finished noting her thoughts, then
wandered into the kitchen to watch Mondo and Sarah
prepare the evening feast. After the maiden placed vessels on the table, she proceeded to push buttons on a
machine to chop an onion. Quinn thought it a compli-

cated way to prepare vegetables.

Next Sarah placed a vessel inside a shiny box with buttons. The food heated in seconds—without fire! Quinn's amazement was unending.

Mondo invited the princess to take a seat at the table. The feast consisted of chopped greens, meat, and cheese wrapped in flat bread. Food in this world was unique. She must remember to mention it in her journal.

In Mandria, she ate a lot of porridge, soups, and stews. Vegetables and fruit came from lush gardens and orchards maintained by Marnies. Meat came from the wild-game forests. The king's hunting party and their dogs rode out daily to bring back fresh meat for Marged's kitchen.

During the repast, conversation between the princess and Sarah was strained. After a final dish of cherries baked inside a pastry, the maiden and her brother departed for another chamber. Quinn remained in the kitchen, desiring time alone with Mondo so she could ask the multitude of questions jumbling through her mind.

"Sire," she began as she helped him put items away and straighten up, "how do you know of the Sign of the Lorik?"

Mondo carried the last vessels from the table to the scullery. He was quiet for so long, Quinn was not sure he'd heard her question. "Mondo?"

He raised a hand to silence her, then held her attention with his pool-colored eyes. "Sometimes it's better not to know too much. This is one of those times." He calmly began to gather empty goblets from the table.

Her face burned. He was her only connection to Mandria; he could *not* shut her out. "Please, Sire, tell me."

"Quinn." Mondo's voice was sharp. His expression told her that *he* knew *she* knew the Mandrian truth she was about to break: *When an elder dismisses a youth, the youth is bound to obey.*

She bowed her head in compliance.

"Now," Mondo added in a lighter tone as he tossed a linen over one shoulder, "go into the living room. There's something in there you might find interesting."

Disappointed, Quinn did as instructed. Adam was sprawled on the cushions, staring at a contraption that resembled a large looking glass. The glass display reflected moving images that seemed to come from inside of it. The princess resisted an urge to examine the back of the object to see where the images were coming from.

Sarah was seated at a desk in front of a similar-looking glass, only hers reflected nonmoving pictures with lots of text. In front of the looking glass was a gadget covered with buttons. Sarah busily tapped on the buttons with all of her fingers at once. The princess had no idea what the device was or why Sarah was so entranced by the words she saw on the glass.

Quinn sank to her knees in front of the object Adam was watching. She saw a large carriage, similar to the school bus, explode and begin to burn.

"What is it?" she asked, covering her face with her hands, not wanting to watch, yet unable to turn her eyes away.

"The evening news."

Adam did not seem bothered at all. With a flick of a wand, he made the alarming noises and the shouting stop. "They're showing clips of a war taking place on the other side of the world."

"Oh, it's terrible," Quinn whispered.

He flicked the wand again. Now the screen displayed children running, laughing, and tumbling over each other, a lot like children in Mandria. The princess watched, hypnotized by the constantly changing images flashing onto the glass.

Mondo joined them. Quinn thought of her family and how, after the evening feast, special guests often gathered around the hearth in the royal tower.

Adam touched her shoulder. "Let's go for a walk. You can wear one of my jackets."

Surprised and pleased by the invitation, Quinn followed him to the portal. As he bundled her into a too-big garment with a large letter *C* on the front, the princess became aware that Mondo was watching them. A quick glance at his face told her he disapproved of the two of them leaving together.

"Don't be gone long," he said in a brusque tone.

Why would he disapprove? Was he trying to protect her? Or Adam? *He might be wiser to disapprove of Sarah's foolishness over Zack.*

Puzzled by Mondo's gruffness, Quinn dared a final glance as Adam opened the door. Mondo's look of disapproval had turned to one of deep, deep sorrow.

13

A Future Set in Stone

~

The princess wrapped Adam's garment tighter around her shoulders, blocking the chilly night air. The change of seasons wasn't as noticeable below the river as it was here. Only in the upper parts of the kingdom could one feel the cold hardness of the earth during fall and winter, and the moist warmness in spring and summer.

Adam kept his arm tight around Quinn as he steered her at a brisk pace. His urgency puzzled her.

Finally they stopped to sit on a low fence surrounding a park dimly lit by lamps on posts. Adam sat in silence for a long moment, then faced her, swinging one leg over the fence as though he were straddling a horse.

"Princess," he began, taking hold of her hands. "How long do you plan to stay with us?"

The question caught her by surprise. Things had

happened so fast since she'd found herself sitting on top of the footbridge, she hadn't had time to consider which she desired most—staying or leaving.

Nor had she thought of the mission with which she'd tried to influence Melikar. The idea of traveling here with a "message" now seemed foolish. Outer-Earth folk had more to teach *her* than she *them*.

Adam's scrutiny was causing the princess great discomfort. Never before had she worried about how she appeared. Proper attire for each royal occasion was based on what had been worn for centuries. Gowns were selected by her ladies—or by Jalla, her former nanny, who made sure the princess's ladies did what they were supposed to do.

Now she found herself longing to be prettier, to own clothes stylish in this world, to cut her hair. Her mind's eye immediately formed the image of an appalled wizard.

Adam nudged her. "Are you going to answer me?"

The princess shook the images from her mind. "I'd planned to visit for only a day and a night, but now . . ."

The wind tousled hair across her face. Adam brushed it back so tenderly, his simple gesture endeared him to her.

"I do not feel comfortable here," she told him. "I miss my parents and Ameka. Cam and Scrabit and—"

"Scrabit?"

"My pet dragon."

Adam reared back in surprise. "You have a pet *dragon*?"

"Yes. A small one. He's a bit bigger than Katze, but

far smaller than the dragons that used to threaten travelers in the outer tunnels."

Adam shook his head. "If I hadn't seen the magic with my own eyes, I would never believe I was sitting here with a princess who owned a magic ring and a pet dragon."

"I guess it seems quite peculiar to you."

"Peculiar isn't even close." He lifted her hand to his lips and kissed her fingers—the way a knight greeted a lady. "I want you to stay with us for as long as you can," he said. "For as long as you want to. You are . . . um . . ." Faltering, Adam watched her face as though he were memorizing it. "You're sweet and gentle . . . and . . . and beautiful," he finished in a whisper.

Quinn shivered at his tender words.

In spite of Adam's presence—and his compliments—talking about Mandria made the princess terribly melancholy. Why was she considering choices at all? Her future did not offer choices. She must return home—and soon—before the king did something drastic, like throw Melikar and Cam into the dungeon.

Her predicament was not their fault. *She* was the one who'd wanted to come to this world. Yet how much lighter her burden would be if she could choose the time and place of her return.

Then there was Adam. The first lad to stir her heart. The first lad to kiss her.

How could she bid him good-bye when there was so much she wanted to know about him?

The princess shifted sideways to face him, boldly

111

placing her arms around his neck. "I cannot stay long in your world," she told him. "I do not know what will happen to me here."

"*Nobody* knows what will happen to them."

"Ay, not true. I know exactly what my life will be—in my world."

"How could you possibly know?"

"It's a Mandrian truth. I'm a princess and an only child. During the season before my sixteenth birthday, the king will host an official coming-of-age ceremony."

"What does that mean?"

"It's an open invitation for all lads of noble blood, from the farthest corners of all the underground kingdoms, to come courting."

The news seemed to vex Adam. "I'm afraid to ask, but what happens next?"

"From all who come, I must choose. A nobleman, a knight, a prince, or perhaps even a king, who meets my father's approval. The castle will immediately prepare for my wedding celebration, which will fall on my birthday or soon after."

"I see," Adam said in a dull voice.

"The king shall proclaim a holiday lasting for three days," she added. "Then, after a wedding trip, I will be expected to bear many grandchildren, especially a son, who will become king when I die."

"Who will rule after your father dies?"

"I'll be queen, since there are no male heirs."

"Wow." Adam whistled beneath his breath. "Amazing."

Cocking his head, he asked, "What if none of the young suitors with noble blood appeals to you?"

The princess loved the way he was gazing at her. She sensed his jealousy, and it made her like him all the more. Afraid to read what his eyes were telling her, she looked away. "If I do not decide in a proper amount of time, the choice will be made for me."

"Bummer."

"Pardon?"

Her words clearly troubled him. "Is that what you want?" he asked. "A blueprinted life with no surprises or unexpected twists?"

Quinn did not know what "blueprinted" meant, but she'd learned long ago not to question her predictable future. "That's the way it is, Adam. It's a—"

"Mandrian truth," he finished, sounding bitter. "The princess marries a nobleman, and they live happily ever under." He gave a weak laugh at his own cleverness.

The lad tried to pull away, but the princess kept her arms tight around his neck. "Upsetting yourself about it makes no sense."

"Why not?"

"Because I do not know how to return to Mandria."

"You don't?"

She thought he sounded pleased. "All I can do is guess."

Adam leaned his forehead against hers. "Then let's not consider your leaving an option."

"But I might be forced to leave."

"Why?"

She hushed her voice. "I sense danger here."

"Danger?" He drew back. "What? Who? Are you in danger?"

"Maybe I am not, but the whole secret of my kingdom's existence is in danger simply by my being here. If the wrong person finds out—" She paused, watching his face.

Adam pulled her close. "I don't want to think about you leaving." His voice sounded trembly. "Everyone I care about . . . leaves."

The princess knew Adam was talking about his parents. She held onto him, as if letting go would break the magic spell they'd woven. Closing her eyes, she asked the High Spirit for relief from the confusion of her predicament. Confusing because, no matter how hard she tried to squelch the truth, her deepest heart told her she'd already chosen the young man who'd caught her fancy.

And the choice frightened the princess so much, she would not allow herself to ponder it.

14

For Lack of
a Spell . . .

~

In the darkness of early morning, a ringing alarm exploded in the middle of the princess's dream.

Sarah was not there to silence the bothersome noise.

Quinn rose from bed and snatched the offending box from a small table. She shook it, but the ringing did not stop.

Katze, snoozing on the window sill, was no help at all. Quinn twisted a knob. The ringing stopped, and music began to play. Music was fine. Much less annoying than a buzzer.

Returning to bed, she curled up again, trying to recall the warm dream from which she'd been rudely yanked. As she willed her mind back inside the mist of the dream world, a feeling of shame flooded her senses. She had been kissing someone!

Adam, of course.

No.

It was *not* Adam.

The lad in her dream was the wizard's apprentice. She had been kissing Cam!

Quinn sat up with an abruptness that startled Katze. Why would she dream such a thing? She missed Cam. He was her childmate, her confidant. Yet in her dream, she had been kissing him the way Adam had kissed her.

The princess's skin grew warm. She touched her face. It felt tender and tight. Getting out of bed, she stumbled to the looking glass above a cabinet. The skin on her face was red. How could it be? Could a shameful dream leave one with a blush that refused to fade?

Worried, the princess put on Sarah's robe and rushed to find her.

She found Adam instead.

"Wow," he said, lifting her chin. "You got sunburned yesterday at the football field."

"Sunburned?" Quinn echoed, relieved to know she was not being permanently punished for her shame.

Adam looked apologetic. "I should've known your skin would burn easily. Guess I'm not taking good care of you like I promised."

Opening a hall cupboard, Adam rummaged through it. "Here's something to make your skin feel better." He gave her a sympathetic look as handed her a bottle of ointment.

Quinn put the remedy into the pocket of her robe and continued on to the kitchen. Sarah and Mondo were at the table, studying large pieces of parchment. They mumbled, "Good morning," but nothing more.

Katze, who'd followed the princess into the kitchen, was the only friendly one. He nudged her leg, purring. She helped herself to a muffin and juice, then carried her morning feast back to Sarah's chamber where she shared bits of the muffin with the cat.

After bathing, Quinn dabbed on the ointment Adam had given her to soothe her burned skin. Today, she did not need to add color to her face with the contents of Sarah's magic pots, although she longed to try the eyelash tint again.

What about garments? Helping herself to Sarah's clothes without asking would only anger the maiden more, so the princess dressed in the same garments she'd worn the day before. Gathering her binder and stylus, she went outside to wait on the front steps for the school bus.

The princess was beginning to feel as out of place as she did during visits to the Marnie village. The hardworking creatures scurried about from early morning until late at night. Quinn never knew where to stand or whether or not it was all right to sit at a workbench. She never knew if she should ask questions or keep silent or if it was proper to pet a Marnie cat—of which they were quite possessive.

The princess thought it odd to be having similar

feelings in this world. If her presence was causing problems, then she simply could not stay. Perhaps she should find somewhere else to lodge. Or was this a sign to go home?

Holding out her hand, she studied Cam's ring. Maybe all she had to do was wish upon the magic. Why hadn't this occurred to her before?

Shoving the binder off her lap, she twisted the ring once.

Wait. Am I truly ready to leave? Should I not first say farewell?

Why? her mind argued. *Sarah wants you gone, and Mondo acts as though he does, too.*

She gave the ring a second twist.

Adam did not want her to leave; she felt sure of that. But wouldn't he be better off if she left now instead of later? Before their feelings for each other deepened? He would understand her urgency to depart without saying good-bye. Wouldn't he?

Taking a deep breath, Quinn twisted the ring a third time.

Closing her eyes, she imagined Mandria: turrets topping castle walls, the coziness of her sleeping chamber; napping with Scrabit until his dragon snores woke her, colorful tapestries covering cold, stone walls.

A tingle shivered through her. She breathed in, smelling the damp earthiness of home.

She heard Marnies trotting along the tunnels.

She saw Melikar gazing into the fire on his hearth.

She pictured herself stepping along the avenues,

wearing her Outer-Earth garments, hair flowing free, eyelashes dark and curled.

Mandrians stopped to point at her and—

"Are you okay?"

Cam! Her heart surged with joy as she opened her eyes.

Adam stepped past her on the stairs. "Let's go," he said. "The bus is waiting."

Quinn's joy traded places with disappointment, then relief. As much as she wanted to go home, part of her could not resist staying here to find out what might happen next. It was almost like living in one of the storybooks Ameka chose for her to read.

The tingle disappeared. Quinn gathered her things, stepping aside on the stairs as Sarah bounded past.

Boarding the bus with the other scholars reminded the princess of the shuttle at WonderLand Park. How quickly she had learned the proper way to act in public.

Adam was sitting with Roger; Sarah sat next to a red-haired lad named Scott. Quinn chose to sit beside a maiden who seemed captivated by the open book in her hand, which was just as well since the princess did not desire to converse with a stranger. Instead, she wanted to ponder why Cam's ring had not worked.

Why were accidental wishes granted, but true wishes were not?

Had she not wished correctly? Or was it fate? Fate could be altered by magic, and magic *had* been sparked by her wish; she'd felt it. Maybe the ring's power was willing but lacked a spell to move her between the two worlds.

The theory made Quinn's heart sink. In the back of her mind, she'd trusted the ring to take her home the instant she was ready. If a spell was necessary, she had bigger troubles than she'd imagined.

How can I conjure a spell? I am not an enchantress. She thought of Cam's words:

> *Anger, fear, love, and mirth.*
> *Send Quinn and Cam to Outer Earth.*

Oddly enough, she'd experienced every one of those emotions since arriving here.

The princess rested her head against the seat. "Is it true, Melikar?" she whispered to herself. "Can I *not* come home of my own accord?"

She bowed her head to hide the tears that threatened to spill down her cheeks.

What have I done? Will I never see my kingdom again?

15

Testing the Magic

~

The morning flow of lessons was uneventful. School-masters and mistresses did not call upon the princess to answer questions—perhaps because she was a new scholar. Still, a heaviness followed Quinn everywhere. Three worries troubled her heart:

One: The ring's magic failed to take her home.

Two: Sarah's heart had closed to her.

Three: Zack.

Yesterday, the princess had relied on the maiden for assistance. Today, locating classrooms by herself was difficult. And everywhere she turned, Zack was there, watching.

Coming to lessons today had been foolish. Her patience was being stretched to its limit.

Toads and mugwort!

Perhaps I cannot choose to return home of my own accord, but I can remain at the Dovers' apartment until Melikar instructs me on how to travel back to Mandria.

It seemed like a good plan until the princess realized she did not know how to return to Mondo's apartment.

Regardless, the mere act of *making a plan* was such a novelty, she had to smile at the intriguing newness of the feeling. Plans were always made *for* her. No one ever asked what *she* felt like doing.

Ay, now I shall do what I desire. It is settled. No more lessons.

Her decision was made shortly before the midday feast, so, to avoid the crowded corridors and noisy cafeteria, she searched until she found the double oak doors in the main hallway and slipped outside.

Even though the princess was hungry, she did not have coins to barter for food. Mondo had given her share to Sarah, but the lass had chosen not to escort her guest today. After each class, Sarah had scurried off before Quinn could catch up with her.

A misty rain began to fall. The princess stepped beneath the branches of a tree for shelter. Leaning against the trunk, she breathed in deeply, experiencing the fresh scent of falling rain for the first time. How much better it would be to have someone with whom to share the moment.

The princess felt as alone as she had in the forest near the footbridge after she realized Cam had not spell traveled with her. Being alone seemed like such a luxury, yet she would not wish for long stretches of it. She'd rather know that Cam was hovering nearby, ready to keep her entertained.

The rain continued as the air turned colder. Shivering, Quinn hugged herself. Instantly, the branches of the tree entwined around her, blocking the chilly wind.

"Thank you," she mumbled, accepting the fact that the tree was sheltering her. She knew it was the tree's dryad, awakened by the surrounding magic, yet she smiled to think how startled an observant passerby might be.

The wood nymph did not answer. Quinn searched the base of the trunk but did not see a maiden's smoky form. Was the aura of magic fading? Did this mean the ring's magic would fade as well?

The idea vexed her. If she hoped to have any protection at all from knaves like Zack, it would have to be by the power of magic. Perhaps she should give the ring a bit of a test?

Ay, for what can I wish that is not frivolous and would not anger the wizard?

The answer came to her at once: food.

Surely Melikar will not begrudge me something to eat.

Twisting the ring, Quinn wished for a piece of fruit.

The familiar tingling shivered through her. A rustling of red and gold leaves drew her attention. In a heartbeat, the branches burst with plump, juicy apples. Pleased, as well as relieved, she plucked a few, feeling grateful that the power in the ring remained strong.

The rain stopped, so the princess spent the rest of the afternoon beneath the tree, reading stories from her lesson books, writing in her journal—and nibbling apples. Toward the end of the day, she gathered her things and returned to the school building, searching until she found the metal compartment in the main corridor that belonged to Adam.

He arrived, looking pleased to find the princess waiting for him. Leaving his books inside the compartment, he took Quinn's hand and escorted her to the large chamber where young folk met to exercise and play sports. The floor was covered with mats on which lads were wrestling.

Adam and Quinn sat on a bench to watch Roger and a boy from another village compete. Adam started to explain the sport to Quinn, but she recognized it as one that was popular with knights and peasants alike in Mandria.

Zack was there, too. He won every match, always looking to see if Quinn was watching. She tried to ignore him, but he put on such a heroic display it was hard not to notice.

The minute Adam left to get something to drink, Zack approached, blocking Quinn's view of the wrestlers.

"Still dating your cousin?" he quipped, watching her face for a reaction.

She did not give him the pleasure of one.

"Everybody knows you two aren't cousins," he added.

"What we *don't* know is why you told everyone you were. Why *did* you?"

Quinn disregarded him, scooting over on the bench until she could view the wrestlers again.

"Well, if you won't answer that, then answer this: Have you pulled any rabbits out of a hat today?"

She would have to ask Adam what that meant.

Zack sat on the bench next to her. "Tell me how you did that trick," he insisted. "The one in the lunch line. And how you shocked me on the bus."

Quinn kept her eyes on the wrestling match, trying not to react.

"Are you magic?" he teased.

Her gaze darted to his. Did he know? Or was he guessing?

Adam returned with Roger, who'd finished his match. The sight of Zack taking his place on the bench next to the princess put a scowl on Adam's face. "What do *you* want?"

Zack stood up, emphasizing his tallness. "Since there's a misunderstanding about who is taking Quinn to the dance," he said, "why don't you and I wrestle tomorrow after school? The winner will, uh, *escort* her." He winked at the princess as if they shared a private joke.

Quinn started to protest, then stopped, not sure if it was acceptable for a maiden to interfere when one lad challenged another.

Adam and Zack glared at each other.

Roger placed a hand on Adam's shoulder. "Not fair,

Zack. Adam isn't on the wrestling team. If you're going to challenge him, make it something neutral."

Quinn glanced from one lad to the other. Their eyes stayed locked in an angry staring match. Her heart boiled with resentment at Zack's unwanted intrusion into her life.

"Fists," Adam suggested calmly.

Zack grinned.

"No!" Quinn exclaimed, not caring if her interruption was proper or not. With mental apologies to Adam, she could plainly see that Zack was stronger.

"What then, little cousin?" Zack asked. "A duel?"

"No!" she said again, not knowing whether or not he was serious.

She blurted the first thing that came to mind. "A jousting match."

All three lads stared at her.

"In the lane behind the school," she added. "If I must attend the ball with the winner, then I shall agree to do so."

Zack looked bewildered at first, then acted indifferent, as though he knew exactly what she was talking about. "I'll be there." He bounded off the benches and stormed away.

Roger raised an eyebrow, giving her a puzzled look. "Excuse me? Would you care to explain *jousting match*?"

Adam groaned. "I, too, would like to know the cause of my future death."

Quinn ignored their jesting. "A jousting match," she told them, "is what everyone suggests when they're challenged."

"Everyone who?" Roger asked.

Was this ritual unknown in the outer world? "Two knights face each other on horseback," she explained. "As they gallop toward each other, both lads try to knock the other off his horse with a lance."

"I was *hoping* that wasn't the kind of jousting you meant." Adam groaned, acting as if she'd embarrassed him. "Horses are a little hard to come by in the 'burbs, and—"

"Wait," Roger interrupted. "I've got a great idea. Let's get going."

After changing clothes, Roger drove them to his cottage. Adam and Quinn sat on the lawn while Roger rounded up a coil of rope and two oars from his father's canoe. They helped him pad the oars with pillows tied with rope. Roger jabbed Adam a few times, trying out the "lances."

"They work, they work." Adam grimaced, holding his stomach. "Now, where are we going to find horses?"

"Wait here." Roger disappeared, returning with two boards on wheels. "Skateboards," he proclaimed. "Twenty-first-century horses."

The lads squared off in the alley behind Roger's house. Quinn clapped her hands to start the match. They charged, flying past her on the skateboards. She hopped to one side as they swished by, barely missing her. Both were hesitant to use the lances on each other.

The princess sat on the ground to watch the competition. The sight of two lads performing an Outer-Earth version of an ancient Mandrian tradition thrilled her—even though these lads tumbled a lot.

After a while, they improved enough to stay on the boards longer. Sore and tired, they made plans to practice once more before the joust, then Roger drove them home, promising he'd fill Zack in on the details of the new sport they'd invented.

In spite of Quinn's worry over Adam's challenge, the princess was secretly pleased to know *she* was the prize for which they jousted. Such was an honor for any Mandrian maiden.

When they arrived home, Mondo had already left for work, and Sarah was in her sleeping chamber. The evening feast still simmered on the stove. Quinn was famished after eating only apples all afternoon.

The meal consisted of flat noodles with a flavorful red sauce. After dining, the princess took her time cleaning the scullery—partly because she'd never done it before and partly to put off confronting Sarah. When finished, she took a deep breath and headed down the corridor to Sarah's chamber.

On the floor outside the portal lay her royal gown in a crumpled heap.

Dismayed, Quinn tapped on the door as she gathered the dress and shook out the wrinkles.

Sarah did not respond, so the princess opened the

door with a hesitant hand. The maiden was working at her writing table.

"May I come in?"

"No," Sarah mumbled, not lifting her head.

Quinn entered anyway and closed the door. "Why are you angry with me?"

Sarah scrunched her face as if she could not believe Quinn had asked such a foolish question. "Why am I angry? You've moved into my room uninvited, helped yourself to my clothes, helped yourself to my boyfriend—"

"Oh, bother," Quinn began, interrupting. "First of all, I thought you *wanted* me to share your room. You offered your clothes—"

"Mondo offered my clothes—*and* my room."

Quinn could not argue; Sarah was correct. She tried again. "If *boyfriend* refers to Zack, I can explain."

"Oh, *sure* you can. You've been flirting with him ever since you got here. Now if he talks to me at all, it's only to ask me about you." She looked as if she were about to cry.

"I did nothing to encourage—"

"You didn't *have* to do anything! He likes you anyway."

Sarah flung a stylus across the room. "Why don't you go back to the weird world you came from?" Stomping to the door, she yanked it open. "You're not sleeping in my room any more. And I want my clothes back, too."

Quinn fled from the chamber, feeling as though she'd been slapped across the face. In this world, being a princess meant absolutely nothing.

She found Adam in front of the moving-picture glass. Still clutching her gown, she slumped beside him on the cushions and told him what had happened.

Adam simply shook his head. "My sister, the drama queen." He pushed a button on the wand in his hand, making the images on the glass change. "Zack is not her boyfriend; she only *thinks* he is. Matter of fact, Scott, the guy with red hair, is crazy about her. Only she doesn't even notice."

"What should I do?" Quinn asked, hearing the quiver in her own voice. "I cannot wear my gown in public, and now I have no place to sleep."

"Yes, you do." Adam pushed another button, causing the glass to blink once then grow dark. "You'll sleep in my room, and I'll kick Katze off the couch and sleep here."

He took the gown from her and hung it in a closet. "I guess now's as good a time as any to take you shopping. Mondo asked why you were wearing the same clothes you wore yesterday, so I filled him in on the way Sarah's been resenting you. He gave me money to buy whatever you want."

Adam fetched a cloak for her, and they went out the door, walking down the avenue until they came to a row of shops. Quinn had never seen so many items for barter in all her life.

In Mandria, there were three types of gowns: formal for balls or cultural events, dressy for pageants or afternoon teas, and simple for morning lessons.

Here, multiple shops overflowed with various garments of many styles and colors. With Adam's guidance, the princess selected a few, plus a pair of shoes. She even purchased her own pots of color for her face and a magic wand for coloring her eyelashes.

On the way home, Quinn kept peeking with delight into the crinkly bags at her earthly purchases. Still, in the back of her mind, a niggling notion told her that Melikar would not approve.

Sighing, she pondered why the invisible wizard held so much power over her thoughts and feelings. She could almost hear his gravelly voice chiding her:

"Mandrian blood flows through your veins, yet the trappings of Outer Earth are drawing you as powerfully as a moth is drawn to a candle's flame . . ."

16

Foiled Plans

The princess felt guilty for taking over Adam's sleeping chamber, but he assured her he would be fine on the "sofa," as he'd called it.

After laying out her new clothes, the princess undressed, pulling a tattered, butter-colored garment of Adam's over her head. It was the only thing she could find in his closet to wear as a sleeping gown.

She hugged it. Having something of Adam's surrounding her made her feel safe.

Taking a tour of his chamber, she studied his possessions: a trophy engraved with his name, the cap with the duck bill he often wore, and a picture of a man and woman. The family resemblance told her it was Adam's father and mother.

Quinn tried to imagine losing her own parents and

hoped the time was long in coming. She admired Adam and Sarah for going on with their lives so bravely, without a mother and father to console their sadnesses and cheer their successes.

Thinking about their family made her think of her own. Homesickness consumed her. Two and a half days had passed, yet the passage of time seemed much longer.

Yawning, she glanced about the chamber for a candle to snuff. Remembering where she was, the princess overlooked her temporary forgetfulness and clicked off the light.

Curling up in Adam's bed was so comforting that the princess soon fell asleep, peaceful for the first time since arriving in this world.

Alas, the pleasant feeling did not last long. Throughout the night, premonitions of danger troubled her dreams. Below the river, premonitions were taken seriously, and Quinn's were usually as accurate as Cam's.

This one had to do with Zack—and the joust, which would take place after lessons ended for the day. The knave was a bully. Bullies lived in the underground world as well and were not trustworthy.

Adam did not have to prove himself to her—or anyone. If he were injured during the joust, she would never forgive herself. The whole thing had been her idea, so she was solely responsible for the lad's safety.

The urgency to warn Adam of her foreboding dream about the unevenly matched joust began to consume her. Rising from bed at first light, the princess hurried to the living chamber where the lad had stayed the night. To her dismay, the room was empty.

Ay, he and Roger planned to meet early this morning to practice jousting one last time. Quinn slumped onto the cushions, feeling defeated. *I shall have to return to the school after all to find Adam and warn him of my dream.*

So much for her plan to remain in the apartment, writing in her journal and exploring the surrounding avenues. Those things would have to wait until tomorrow.

Although the princess had not adjusted to tight-fitting garments or unbraided hair, dressing in her own earthly clothes was pleasurable. Adam had purchased ornaments to keep locks of hair from falling across her face. Taking the clips out of the package, she fastened one behind each ear.

The princess tried to apply the eyelash magic in the tiny looking glass above Adam's writing table, but soon realized how difficult it was. Sarah had done it effortlessly. *Sarah.*

A heaviness settled over the princess. She missed the lightheartedness she and Sarah had shared the first day. *How can I mend our rift when I have not done anything wrong?*

Oh, bother. If only the lass could see the truth.

The princess took her time preparing to leave. She dreaded boarding the school bus again and fleetingly wondered if the magic ring might whisk her to school at once so she would not have to face Mondo and Sarah this morning. But she knew better. She desired to please Melikar and not worry him—especially if he was watching her.

Picking up her new outer garment, intended to be worn outdoors like a cloak, she headed for the kitchen. Sarah's friend, Scott, leaned against a cabinet, waiting to escort the maiden to school.

"Morning," Quinn said, smiling at him.

Before the lad could answer, Sarah grabbed his arm. "Come on, I'm ready." She glowered at Quinn as the two hurriedly left the apartment.

Quinn sat at the table, feeling overwhelmed before the day had barely begun. *Did Sarah think I was being coquettish with Scott merely by saying hello?*

Frustrated, she wished she could shake some sense into the maiden. Scott and Zack were of no interest to her. All she cared about right now was Adam—and what was going to happen this afternoon in the pathway behind the school—what had Roger called it? The "alley."

Mondo entered the kitchen, carrying a roll of parchment. "Good morning, dear one," he said as he poured a cup of tea. His smile was cheerful, which lifted Quinn's spirits enormously.

Mondo filled her goblet with juice, then served her a pastry with bilberry jam. "I was planning to ask your opinion of this world, now that you've had a couple of days to sample it." He peered at her over the top of his spectacles. "From the look on your face, I'd guess your opinion isn't too optimistic."

Quinn dipped her finger into the jam to taste it. She thought it not as flavorful as bilberry jam made by her nanny, Jalla.

"Lessons are fine," she told Mondo. "Quite interesting, actually, yet so different from my formal instruction in Mandria. But . . ." Pausing, she glanced at Mondo, hesitant to complain to him about his own granddaughter. "I'm having difficulties with Sarah, and—"

"I know," Mondo interrupted. "Adam informed me. Sarah is used to being the only princess around here, if you'll pardon the expression. She's never quite recovered from the loss of her parents."

He took a sip of tea and appeared to ponder his own comment. "Adam has handled the aftermath of the accident much better than his sister, but then, he's older. Sarah has our love and patience, but she's never had to share us with anyone. Since you arrived, Adam has practically ignored her—not intentionally, of course, but I can tell Sarah has been unhappy these past few days."

Mondo helped himself to a pastry. "Adam will soon be leaving for college. I worry that his departure will be another great loss for his sister."

Mondo's words made Quinn feel remorseful about her impatience with Sarah. Zack was obviously not the only issue that had set the maiden against her. She believed Quinn was stealing her brother away as well. *Ay, biddle*, as Jalla would say.

The princess silently promised the High Spirit she would try harder to make amends with the impatient lass.

Mondo spread the large pages of parchment onto the table. "Other than the disharmony between you and my granddaughter, is everything else all right?"

Now was her chance to question Mondo's irregular behavior toward her. She straightened in her chair. "No, everything else is *not* all right."

The princess waited for him to meet her gaze. "My being here bothers you as strongly as it does Sarah. Why, Sire?"

Mondo seemed startled by her direct question. His blue-green eyes clouded as he placed a wrinkled hand on her arm. "Forgive me, child, if I've made you feel unwanted. You are *more* than welcome to share our home."

He hesitated, as if his next words were painful to express. "I only wish you would not spend so much time with my grandson."

His comment perplexed her. "But why? Adam and I truly care for each other."

Mondo's hand jerked away. He rose with such abruptness, the juice in Quinn's goblet spilled. Swiftly he gathered the parchment from the table and turned to leave.

With his back to her, he said, "If I could be Melikar for one brief moment, I'd cast such a powerful spell over you and Adam, you would never be able to bear the sight of one another."

17

Rainbows and Deceptions

~

All the way to school, Mondo's words hung heavy in Quinn's heart. He was hiding something from her.

But what? Why would he desire to keep her and Adam apart? And what was his connection to her world?

Today's gloomy chill made Quinn grateful for the outer garment Adam had bought her. A "jacket" he had called it. In Mandria, the air was the same every day. How difficult it would be to grow accustomed to the air changing every day. How could proper garments be chosen?

Over the course of two days, the princess had felt the warmth of the sun and the damp coolness of rain. Today, a gray blanket covered the sky, blocking the sun. The closeness of this "ceiling" made her feel more at home than the wide openness of the endless heavens, yet she did not care to look at a sky the color of woodsmoke after seeing how gloriously blue it could be.

"Weather" was a topic she heard discussed frequently, yet weather did not even exist in her world. The sameness of the underground climate was comforting, albeit boring.

Another thing the princess did not care for today: being at school after deciding to be finished with the bother of it all. She had come solely for Adam's sake. The sooner she found the lad and warned him to cancel the joust, the sooner she could depart. Until then, she might as well attend lessons, which, she admitted, were interesting.

Unfortunately, she was not allowed to remain in the first class until the headmaster contacted Mondo to approve the previous day's absence. She was given a note of entry to present in each class thereafter, which drew attention she did not desire. Was protocol in this world as stifling as protocol beneath the river?

At midday, the princess sought reprieve from noisy scholars and the strain of having to watch her words and actions. She found her way to an enclosed courtyard. Stone benches were scattered beneath trees that resembled buttonball trees in the queen's garden. Glass walls enclosed the courtyard. Sitting on one of the benches, Quinn watched the parade of students on the other side of the glass. The moment she spotted Adam she would dash back inside to talk to him.

Moments later, the princess caught sight of Roger waving in an exaggerated manner. He worked his way against the flow of young folk in the corridor and stepped outside to join her.

"Hey," he said, setting his knapsack of books on a path that wound through the dropberry bushes. "Are you crazy, coming out here to sit in the mist and the fog?"

"Yes," she answered, returning his smile. She hoped the simple answer staved off a truthful explanation for why she was here—which, of course, he would never believe.

Awkward silence filled the courtyard as she tried to think of topics of conversation. *Ay, I shall ask Roger the question I've heard others asking all day, even though I do not know what it means.*

"What are you going to be for Halloween?"

"Didn't Adam tell you?" he asked, which told her that her question had made perfect sense to him. "After our jousting practice, I found a picture of two knights in armor with real lances. I showed it to my girlfriend, Wendy, and she made costumes for us. So we'll be going to the dance as knights."

"Knights!" Quinn repeated, pleased by his answer. The thought of Adam dressed as a knight gave her chills. She imagined the lad riding a handsome steed through the castle gates to ask the king's permission to court her.

"So, m'lady," Roger jested, "you may call me Sir Roger." Placing one foot in front of the other, he bowed low with a flourish of his arm. "What are *you* going to be for Halloween?"

The princess had deduced by the conversation that

"what are you going to be?" referred to costumes. She loved finding similarities between the worlds, and here was another. Apparently, costume balls were lavish events both above and below the river.

Jalla would sew whatever sort of costume the princess desired. Cydlin and Gwynell would dash madly about, searching for the perfect accessories to make the costume authentic.

But here? What sort of costume could she create without the help of Jalla or her ladies?

Perhaps a royal sapphire gown with jeweled slippers will do . . .

"I think I shall be a princess," Quinn told him, trying to sound as if the idea just occurred to her—which, indeed, it had.

Roger glanced at an object strapped around his wrist. Quinn had seen many people do this and wondered why. "Hey, the bell's about to ring," he said. "We'd better get inside."

Reluctantly, she followed Roger toward the door, still thinking about Adam as a knight. Why could fate not allow him to be one of the noble lads coming to the castle to court her before her sixteenth birthday? Perturbed by the unfairness, she glanced at the sky before stepping inside. A few clouds had parted. In between curved a hazy arch, shimmering in colorful stripes.

"Ay, look!" Quinn exclaimed, pointing skyward.

Roger stepped back outside and followed her gaze.

"Oh, a rainbow." He shrugged, holding the door

open for her, but she continued to stare at the sky.

"Rainbow?" she repeated.

He gave her a puzzled look as if unsure whether or not she was jesting. "You act like you've never seen one before."

His words reminded her to act "normal." Tearing her gaze away, she ducked inside, even though she longed to stay and see what happened to the hazy sky-colors.

Why did Melikar tell me this world holds no magic?

The princess attended all of her afternoon lessons, never once spotting Adam in the corridor as she had the day before. The final bell reminded her of what was to happen in the alley after school. Urgency from her premonition returned like a winter fever—and she still hadn't warned Adam.

Jousting matches in Mandria were sometimes fought to the death. Quinn shivered at the memory of one that ended in tragedy. She was a young lass at the time but knew the match had been held to decide who would win the hand of a maiden named Gwynnith.

During the joust, both knights were fatally injured. The maiden, in her sorrow, departed to live in the Kingdom of Banyyan, yet on her way, was kidnapped by rogue Tristans and was never seen again.

Filled with dark thoughts, Quinn hurried away from her last class—and smashed squarely into Mr. French.

"There you are!" the schoolmaster exclaimed, recovering his spectacles, which had gone flying across the corridor when they collided. "I've been looking for you." He adjusted a stack of red-penciled papers. "You must go immediately to the office. The admissions office has been unable to locate your school records."

Quinn froze in her deception.

"It's quite odd actually," Mr. French continued. "They say the computer has no history of you whatsoever, as though you don't even exist. But computers have been known to chew up records and swallow them whole, so I'm not surprised at the mix-up. However, they do wish to speak with you, and—"

"Not now," Quinn blurted, backing away. "I have an appointment. I'll have my grandfather—I mean—" Quinn stopped, confused about what to call Mondo.

Mr. French shook his head. "Don't delay, Miss Mandria. This must be straightened out at once. You're not officially enrolled until all of your records have been transferred. This is highly irregular."

The princess tried again to give a correct answer. "I'll have Grandfather Dover call the headmaster and explain."

Mr. French shoved on his spectacles, grumbled about students "bending rules at will," and then shuffled down the corridor.

Relief and annoyance filled Quinn at the same time. School protocol and "missing" records were the least of her worries. Right now, she needed to fortify herself for another battle with Zack—and with Adam mixed up in it this time.

As much as she wanted to warn the lad, part of her sensed she was too late. How could she expect Adam to do what no knight in Mandria would do? Turn his back on a challenge and walk away.

Was this Mandrian truth also an Earthly truth? If so, the possible consequences frightened the princess even more than having her secret revealed.

18

A Misguided Token of Luck

~

Quinn hurried out the nearest door and made her way to the alley behind the school. The frigid air almost took away her breath.

Dashing around a brick wall, she came to an abrupt stop at the sight before her. Dozens of young folk filled the alley—half surrounding Adam and Roger, and half surrounding Zack.

Stunned, she had not considered the arrival of spectators. Word of the joust must have spread through the school as fast as news of which couple had begun to court and which had ended their courtship.

The princess searched the crowd for Sarah, but the maiden did not appear to be present.

Indeed not, Quinn told herself.

How could Sarah cheer for either Adam or Zack with

the princess as the trophy? Sarah would be wise to ignore the whole situation.

The sea of jostling bodies separating Quinn from Adam dismayed her. In Mandria, crowds parted to let the princess pass the moment she appeared.

Fighting her way toward Adam, she grabbed the sleeve of his jacket. "Please, we need to talk!" she shouted over the noise.

He followed her to the other side of the brick wall. "What's the matter? Is something wrong?"

"Do not do this," she pleaded.

"Why not?" He calmly adjusted the "baseball catcher's chest protector" he'd promised her he would wear.

This was not the best moment to explain Mandrian premonitory dreams to him. "You do not have to prove anything," she said instead. "Zack cannot keep you from courting me. This is foolish."

Adam studied her face and frowned. "Are you implying that I'm going to lose? No way. Roger and I practiced for hours. I've gotten pretty good and—"

Quinn clutched his arm. "It is more than practice." How could she say it without hurting his feelings? "Strength has a lot to do with it, and you and Zack are . . . mismatched."

His eyes told her she'd chosen the wrong words.

"You think Zack is stronger? More athletic? You think he's going to whip me?"

She did not answer, which agitated him further.

"So, you want me to back down like a coward?"

His reply told her that, yes, challenges were the same in both worlds. Adam's pride would not allow him to turn back.

Neither would the excited crowd.

He shoved his hands into heavy gloves.

"Gee, Princess, thanks for the vote of confidence. If Zack is so much more of a man, then I'm sure you'll enjoy being his girlfriend instead of mine."

"Please do not be angry . . . I had a premonition."

Shrugging as if he didn't care, he turned away.

Ignoring Mandrian premonitions was dangerous. But, of course, he would not know this.

As Adam edged his way through the wall of young folk, they began to chant for the joust to commence.

The princess wound through the crowd to follow him. "I do not trust Zack," she called. "He means you harm."

Adam continued on.

Quinn's throat burned as the urge to cry overwhelmed her. She had not meant to wound the lad's feelings. Why had he taken her warning the wrong way?

Roger was trying to control the crowd, making the scholars back away to one side or the other to give the jousters room. As Adam knelt in the center to pull on pads for his knees, the princess caught up with him.

"There's one more thing," she told him.

He raised skeptical eyes to her. Quinn whispered close to his ear. "A lady always gives her knight a token of luck to take into a joust. It's a Mandrian truth." As she spoke, she realized she had no scarf, handkerchief, or ribbon—the usual token.

Adam rose at the urging of the crowd. She thought he looked pleased by her words as he waited to see what she would offer him.

As she searched for a token, her eyes fell upon the magic ring. Yes! It would make a fine token of luck, and besides, it was all she had to offer. Twisting it off her finger, she grabbed his gloved hand. "Here, m'lord, for luck."

Adam stared at the ring, then looked at her with hurt and bewilderment on his face. "I don't need magic to help me win. I'd rather depend on skill."

Roger stepped up, interrupting them. "Don't forget your batting helmet," he said, handing Adam a round object.

"But it's merely a token, and—"

Adam shoved the ring back into her hand. He pulled on the helmet, then grabbed the "lance" from Roger. As he raised the lance above his head, cheers exploded from the crowd.

"And what?" he asked her. "Zack might kill me? Is that what you were going to say?" He pursed his lips in disappointment. "If I die, Your Highness, bury me beneath the river so I'll be near you forever."

His sarcasm wounded her heart.

Zack began to yell obscenities at them for stalling.

Planting the skateboard, Adam sailed across the alley in his opponent's direction.

Quinn's stomach churned as she watched him. How could he plunge into this joust angry with her? She had not meant to insult him. Some truths simply did not translate between worlds.

He and the knave were an unbalanced match. In Mandria, such was an invitation to death.

Zack sailed into the crowd on Adam's side of the alley, scattering spectators. He swooped close to the princess, making her flinch.

The lad tipped his skateboard to stop it. She was the one he was after. Grabbing the princess around the waist, he pulled her roughly to him, drawing everyone's attention. The strong smell of spirits gagged her as his mouth covered hers with a sloppy kiss.

Quinn wrenched free, wiping her mouth as her eyes searched for Adam. She caught the pained expression on his face as he turned away.

Zack threw back his head and howled like a crazed wolf. Sailing across the alley, he shouted for the joust to begin.

19

Reading the
Fire

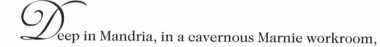

Deep in Mandria, in a cavernous Marnie workroom,
Cam put the finishing touches on a new magic ring.

He'd shaped the ring from gold scraps given to him
by Grizzle, a wizened Marnie who'd taught him how to
form objects out of precious metals.

Cam glanced up to see if Grizzle was charting his
progress.

He was.

The fur circling the Marnie's head was as full as a
lion's mane. When he nodded his approval, the fur
shimmered golden-red in the firelight.

Picking up the ring with a pair of tongs, Cam thrust
it one last time into a fire pit. The heat would soften the
metal, allowing him to correct a slight imperfection in
the curve of the band.

He was careful not to leave his creation in the fire too long, otherwise the markings he had engraved earlier would melt.

Grizzle shifted impatiently.

Cam knew how hard it was for the old one to watch him work without snatching the ring away and finishing it himself. Dropping the band into a bowl of cold water to cool, Cam waited as steam rose into the air.

He no longer wondered what happened to his first ring. Melikar told him it had traveled to the other world with the princess. The wizard was highly displeased with her attempts to use the magic.

Cam shivered at the thought. Surely she knew better. Even he, with his limited ability, knew the dangers of naively dabbling in magic. They'd both listened to Melikar's lectures too many times for her *not* to know it.

According to the wizard, Quinn was not being selective with the ring's magic. Granted, she'd been exposed to enchantments many times in Mandria, but she'd never held such power in her own hands.

Cam remembered the first time Melikar allowed him to cast a spell. The sense of power was overwhelming. He imagined how much greater that power would seem to an unenchanted person.

His mind flashed to the dream about the princess and her pursuer. He hoped she *would* resort to magic if she found herself in danger.

Grizzle poked him in the side, yanking his thoughts to the present task.

Reaching into the cold water to recover the ring, Cam shook it dry as he slipped the ornament onto his first finger. He studied it with pride. This ring was better than the other. He'd taken more time to create it.

Was it possible to cast a spell to make its magic stronger? He'd try.

"Perfect." He grinned at Grizzle, giving the Marnie a pat on top of his bald spot.

Grizzle slapped his hand away, acting annoyed with Cam for distracting him from his own work, yet Cam knew the Marnie welcomed his projects.

Shooing two sleeping kittens off his worktable, Grizzle returned to his chore of shaping goblets out of molten metal.

Hurrying from the Marnies' cramped chambers, Cam was eager to be away from the heat of the fire pits and back to the wide, airy avenues of upper Mandria. He rubbed his throat, irritated now from wood smoke.

As he followed the tunnels, lit by enchanted daylight, he wished he could use the ring to whisk himself to Melikar's chamber, avoiding the lengthy hike home. But until he cast the spell to make the ring *magic*, it was nothing more than an ordinary piece of jewelry.

When Cam arrived at Melikar's chamber, Ameka was there.

She came frequently now, since extra time filled her days—time usually spent tutoring the princess.

Melikar sat in his oak rocker, staring at the fire on his hearth.

Ameka's amber gown ballooned around her as she knelt beside the wizard and began to plead with him.

Cam stopped at the portal to listen. No one was allowed to disturb Melikar when he was reading the fire. Did Ameka not know this?

Before Cam could warn her, Melikar spoke.

"It is useless to ask me to send you to the other world."

"But, Sire," Ameka argued, "if the princess does not know how to return, you must teach me the spell, then send me to her so I can bring her safely home."

The enchanter remained silent, gazing into the crackling flames.

"Melikar," Ameka said, her voice rising in apprehension. "She's been gone almost a quarter moon's turn."

"I know how long it's been."

Cam knew his master was also concerned about the spell he'd cast on the king and queen. Presently, they sat in the royal tower, as silent and still as statues, the pot of enchanted tea long grown cold.

Doleran seeds worked for only a limited time. Continuing their use was dangerous to one's heart.

Ameka glanced at Cam, acknowledging his presence. "What harm could possibly come from my traveling to the other side of the pool?"

Melikar's gaze shifted from the fire to Ameka. "It could cause insurmountable harm. Already one Mandrian maiden is lost in the other world on my account." His eyes moved to take in Cam, whose remorse over the whole situation had not diminished. "Why would I allow another Mandrian to travel unprotected to the other side—engaging in spells and charms far beyond her knowledge and ability?"

Ameka bowed her head, yielding to the elder's decision. It was a Mandrian truth.

Melikar dismissed her with a turn of his head.

She rose, nodding at Cam as she passed.

The only sound in the chamber was the popping of the fire and the creak of Melikar's rocker. Then, in a soft voice, as if nothing had occurred to upset him, the wizard spoke again.

"Cam, Ameka, come join me and I will tell you of Princess Quinn's sojourn in the other world."

The two exchanged excited glances. Both were at the bursting point with worry and curiosity over what was happening to their princess.

Eagerly, they sat at Melikar's feet, waiting while he continued his somber reading. After a length of time, with Cam nearly ready to remind him they were waiting, the wizard began to speak.

"Quinn is well taken care of. She is staying with a family and has gone to lessons wearing borrowed garments. She has quickly adapted to life in the other world." He paused to sigh. "Too quickly, I'm afraid."

"Is she happy?" Ameka stared wide-eyed into the fire, as if trying to see what the wizard saw.

"I'm afraid not," replied Melikar. "Her visit has been full of strife."

"Over what?" she asked, looking quite concerned.

Cam, whose emotions ranged far beyond concern, leaned in closer to better hear what the wizard was about to say.

"Conflicts abound," Melikar continued, "with the maiden whose home she shares and with the grandfather, both over different lads."

"*Two* Outer-Earth lads?" Ameka clapped her hands, looking pleased.

Cam shifted in discomfort. He had not considered the fact that the princess would meet—and certainly charm—lads in the other world.

Of course they would notice her—she is beautiful. Needles of jealousy pricked his heart.

Squinting into the fire, he wished his magic was as powerful as Melikar's. Sometimes he could see faint pictures in the flames, but he did not know how to interpret them. Rising to his knees, Cam tried to shake off the uneasy sensations troubling him. "Is the princess in danger?"

"Yes. She's in great danger," Melikar answered. "And so is the whole existence of our kingdom." His voice wavered. "Quinn is using the magic unwisely. She should not be using it at all."

Cam studied the wizard's drawn face, wondering if he should mention the perilous dream that haunted his sleep.

Melikar focused on his apprentice. "It would be better for us all if your ring had remained in Mandria instead of traveling to the other world with the princess."

Cam sensed a shudder trembling through Melikar as he continued. "Lad, you must use your power of suggestion to instruct Quinn how to come home. You must meditate as often as you can upon this. Do you understand?"

"But, Sire, *your* power is much greater than mine."

"Ay, your words are true, lad, but the princess resists every hint I send, as though she knows it's coming from me. I am accustomed to her stubbornness, because she reacts the same way whenever she visits my chamber—ignoring what she does not want to hear. You seem better able to reach her than I."

The wizard placed a hand on Cam's shoulder. "Try, lad."

"Yes, Master."

Perhaps there was no need to mention his dream to Melikar. Could the wizard be having the same nightmare? On the other hand, perhaps the dream came only to him, as his hints to the princess were the only ones to penetrate her mind.

Either way, telling Melikar was pointless. He already knew the princess was in danger.

Cam bade Ameka and the wizard good-night, then retired to his cot in the corner. Why waste time? The princess needed his help.

Closing his eyes, he relaxed, focusing on Quinn, trying to envision her in the strange garments he'd seen Outer-Earth maidens wearing at the wishing pool.

Cam recalled each step in the spell to return to

Mandria and imagined them again and again. He even pretended he was sitting with Quinn in the queen's garden beneath a buttonball tree, telling her in person:

> *Return to the wishing pool.*
> *Stand on the crest of the footbridge.*
> *Wish with all your heart to return to Mandria.*
> *Pivot to initiate the whirlpool.*
> *Once it forms, allow yourself to be drawn into it.*
> *Do not resist the pull of the magic.*

Yet every time Cam listed the steps, his concentration slipped. First, because his irritated throat had worsened, and the pain kept seeping into his consciousness. And second, he could not ignore the knowledge that Quinn had suitors in the other world.

Taking a deep breath, the apprentice renewed his efforts to focus on the princess and the spell. In the morning, he would ask Melikar to mix a healing potion of slippery elm and white oak bark with a pinch of balanyn in honey to soothe his throat.

And in the morning, he would worry about the Outer-Earth lads who had taken a romantic interest in his princess.

20

Twenty-First-Century Joust

~

The princess held her breath while the jousters squared off, facing each other. Crowds on both sides of the alley backed away and gave them room.

The lads resembled Tristans from the Valley Kingdom. Tristans dressed in outlandish costumes and carried unusual lances. Roger had invented a more streamlined version of a lance than the oars and pillows. These were broomsticks, cushioned with something he called "foam."

Zack wore the oversized shoulders and padded knees the princess had seen him wear while chasing a ball around the meadow. Adam wore part of a cage over his face. Padding hung from each shoulder, like a knight's breastplate. On his head sat a cap similar to the duckbill one he always wore, only made of hard material.

The crowd hushed.

In position, Adam and Zack stood motionless, lances held high.

Roger, the moderator, explained the challenge to the crowd: "The jouster who knocks his opponent off the skateboard two out of three times is the winner."

Quinn held her breath while Roger pressed two fingers to his lips and gave a shrill whistle.

Instantly, the crowd came to life as the two lads shoved off on planks with wheels that Roger called "skateboards."

Adam's hours of practice showed. He knew precisely how fast to push his skateboard, at what angle to hold his lance, and when to give it a powerful thrust.

It worked.

The blow caused Zack to lose his balance on the first pass. He fell hard but quickly rolled and came to his feet.

Adam's side of the alley cheered while Zack's side booed.

Quinn slowly released the breath she'd been holding. She'd been wrong about Adam. He knew what he was doing. Skill *could* win over strength.

The princess relaxed as the lads sailed past each other a few times. *For show,* she thought, *exactly like knights in Mandria.*

The cheering crowd and exciting competition made her almost feel as though she were at a true joust. Granted, no horses pranced by, splendid in colorful trappings. Ladies were not dressed in gowns, nor knights in chain mail with shields displaying their family crest.

Another difference came to mind as well. Zack was angry. Furious. In an actual joust, a knight did not show emotion, whether winning or losing. Any kind of reaction would bring him disgrace. It was a Mandrian truth.

The back of Quinn's neck warmed as Zack hurled insults at Adam—who did not respond to his opponent's abuse. Adam's face remained set with concentration. The princess was proud of the lad for keeping his temper, thus keeping his honor.

As Zack became more verbal, so did the crowd. Passes on the skateboards became faster and more reckless.

Zack was on guard now, fending off blows from Adam's lance. He had not yet tried to strike.

For what was he waiting? A gnawing feeling of uneasiness crept over the princess. She did not trust Zack any more than she trusted a band of renegade Tristans. They'd look you straight in the eye while robbing your gold.

As the lads made another pass, Zack knocked Adam's lance off-target, as before, but this time he leaned into Adam, bumping him off the skateboard with his oversized shoulders.

Adam sprawled on the ground. His skateboard sailed off into the crowd.

Zack zigzagged a little but recovered. His supporters roared their approval.

Adam awkwardly pulled himself to his feet, constricted

by the heavy garb. He watched Roger, waiting for him to intervene, to disqualify the hit as unfair. No lance was used.

Quinn cringed. Ay, Roger had not told the crowd any rules other than how a jouster claimed victory. He could not, therefore, claim the hit did not count.

Adam searched out the princess and locked gazes with her for a few seconds. His frown told her he shared her thoughts. He probably wished she had discussed the rules more thoroughly with Roger.

Still, it came as no surprise that Zack would not let rules stand in his way of winning. Quinn refused to watch his disgusting display of triumph—circling his lance above his head, shouting of his own greatness.

The crowd began to chant, "Zack, Zack, Zack, Zack."

The princess twisted the magic ring. If Zack could bend the rules, than why couldn't she? All the horrid things she was empowered to wish upon the lad gave a devilish tickle to her imagination.

What shall I do to him?

She imagined the shock of the crowd if Zack suddenly turned into a frightened mouse, skittering down the alley to hide. Quinn was surprised at how fabulous the idea of being wicked to Zack made her feel.

Adam circled in front of her, completing another pass. As their eyes met, she had difficulty reading his emotions. His final words echoed in her mind. *I don't need magic to help me win; I'd rather depend on skill.*

Sighing, she knew she had to honor his words. She could not call upon the ring's magic. Adam would never forgive her. The humiliation of being saved by a maiden would be too much to bear.

Discouraged, the princess faded back into the crowd, not wanting to witness the rest of the joust. Anything could happen now that the score was tied.

The tension in the air was as thick as the young folk pressing close to see better. Quinn retreated to the brick wall, allowing others to step in front and block her view. She could not breathe.

Please let Adam win, she implored the High Spirit.

The thought of Zack's victory turned her heart to ice. How could she bring herself to attend the ball with him as an escort?

Sarah already hated her because of Zack, and now Adam would hate her because of him, too. Why had this evil lad come into her life and spoiled her journey?

The crowd became still and silent as the jousters *whooshed* past each other, again and again, building anticipation.

Quinn could not bear to watch, yet *not* watching was torture. Stepping upon a low windowsill, she balanced on her toes to see over the crowd. As she watched Adam, her heart soared with pride. His skill was impressive.

Zack gave up on the verbal abuse and fell silent, as if he needed all his concentration for the last point.

The rhythmic roll of wheels on the hard surface of the alley seemed to mesmerize the crowd. Adam sailed to the far end of the alley and made a wide turn to start back. A moment before the pass, Zack swerved directly into Adam's path.

Anticipating a head-on crash, Adam flinched, jerking his skateboard to the right while Zack turned smoothly away, keeping perfect balance.

Adam tried to recover but skidded sideways and fell into the crowd.

Zack had cheated again! Quinn's emotions broke, bringing tears. The unfairness of it all made her want to give Zack a few angry jabs with a real knight's lance.

Quickly she wiped away the tears and burrowed back into the crowd, needing to find Adam and console him. Half the young folk were cheering for the victor—the other half protesting the unfair match.

Poor Roger. He'd have to justify the unclear rules. The confusion was more her fault than his. She should not have been so quick to simplify Mandrian jousting customs.

Quinn circled through the crowd twice, but Adam was no longer there. Her knight had ridden off on his twenty-first-century horse. She did not blame him for leaving to nurse his wounds alone.

"Hey!" Zack hollered, sailing toward her on his skateboard. "Come kiss the winner." He pulled off his helmet and grinned at her.

Quinn stifled an unprincess-like urge to slap his smirking face.

He circled her. "I guess you're all mine for the *ball,* as you call it." He slid to a stop in front of her, hopping off his board. "What happened to your ride home? The loser afraid to show his face?" He took her arm as he picked up his skateboard. "No problem. I'll take you home."

"No, you won't," came Roger's voice from behind. "She's riding with me."

Quinn almost hugged Adam's friend in relief. Yanking her arm from Zack's grasp, she hurried away with Roger.

But not fast enough to miss Zack's departing growl, loud enough to scorch her royal ears:

"Tomorrow, little cousin. Tomorrow is the match between you and me."

21

The Princess's Choice

Morning crept into Adam's room, waking the princess from her dream about Cam. The apprentice seemed frantic to inform her of something of extreme importance, but she could not concentrate on his words because her throat felt irritated and sore.

Swallowing, she flinched in pain.

If she were in Mandria, she'd ask Melikar to mix his healing potion of slippery elm, white oak bark, . . . and whatever herb made the magic work. She'd forgotten its name.

Shaking the dream from her mind, she wondered if Adam ever came home last night. She'd waited for him until she could no longer stay awake.

Sarah had come in early from her tryst with Scott but went directly to her chamber and closed the door.

Quinn sat up, smoothing her tangled hair. How was she supposed to make it through the day? *And tonight's Halloween ball*, her memory added, bringing her fully awake. Sighing, she wondered why everything couldn't go back to the way it was before.

Before Zack.

The princess dressed in new leggings she now knew were called "jeans." How uncomfortable they'd felt the first time she'd worn Sarah's, but now she rather liked them and wished they were fashionable below the river. They seemed sensible for Mandrian maidens to wear in the cool, damp air. Running and climbing rocks in the grotto would be easier, too—granted, she was no longer supposed to do such things . . .

Quinn put on a soft, blue garment Adam had chosen from one of the shops. Blue was his favorite color, he'd told her. Maybe if he saw her wearing it today, he would not be so angry with her.

Adam.

She hurried into the living chamber. He was not there. He wasn't anywhere in the apartment. Maybe he had left early with Roger. To avoid her?

Sarah was gone as well. She'd been riding to school with Scott instead of taking the bus.

Mondo was absorbed by what he called the morning news and did not have much to say. When she complained about her throat, he offered a tumbler of water and two button-like objects to swallow. She wondered if his medicine worked as well as Melikar's potion for inflamed throats.

So much for her plan to stay at the apartment. Yesterday, she had to go to school because of the joust. Today, finding Adam was crucial. She needed to mend their misunderstanding and reassure him of her affection and loyalty—before going off to the ball with Zack.

Mondo was concerned over her ill health. He offered to take her to school in his carriage so she would not have to face a noisy bus ride. She gladly accepted.

What met her eyes when she arrived at the gray stone building was a shock.

Scholars were dressed in bizarre outfits. One lad sprouted purple hair; another had no hair at all. Unfamiliar eyes gazed through masks of monster faces, animals, or distorted humans.

One scholar wore a bedsheet over his head with holes cut out for eyes. Another oozed blood from a knife protruding from his forehead. Quinn hoped it was trickery.

The gaiety in the corridors lifted her spirits, making her realize how long it had been since anything had caused her to laugh.

She stepped into a girls' room to comb her hair. Only a few days had passed since she and Sarah had shared amusement here in front of the looking glass, yet so much had changed since then.

Two maidens entered. Quinn finished brushing her hair, then pretended to brush it once more so she could listen to their conversation—and stare at their odd clothes. One was dressed as a green-faced hag, ugly as any below the river. The other was a mouse, complete with a long tail, rounded ears, and whiskers.

The maidens were plotting to *cut* homeroom so they could *cram* for a first-period exam. Quinn was unsure what *cut* or *cram* meant, yet she could translate the meaning. Not going to homeroom sounded like a wonderful idea—the *last* person she wanted to run into was Mr. French. Surely he would send her to the headmaster's chamber to explain the whereabouts of her nonexistent records.

Perhaps she could tell the headmaster that the information did not exist because she'd employed a private tutor all her life. And if he wished to contact the tutor, all he had to do was wrap a letter around a stack of coins, address it to "Ameka of Mandria," then heave it into the wishing pool at WonderLand Park.

As the "mouse and hag" departed from the girls' room, the princess gave them a silent "thank you" for the idea to avoid lessons since the sole purpose for her presence today was to locate Adam.

Feeling daring, yet guilty for breaking rules, Quinn stepped into the corridor and hurried toward the library— the opposite direction of homeroom. Spending most of the day in the quiet room would give her plenty of time to record her thoughts and impressions in the journal.

The unexpected day of costumes kept the princess entertained during class breaks when she returned to the corridors to search for Adam.

At midday, she persuaded a maiden to lend her a pig-head mask that sported long eyelashes and blond hair. The lass warned Quinn that masks must be removed during lessons, but that did not concern the princess. Eagerly, she twisted her hair into a knot in order to don the mask and, in disguise, walked passed both adversaries—Zack and Mr. French—yet neither noticed her.

Was Adam hiding behind a mask, too? Was that why she could not find him after searching the entire day? Or had he not come to lessons at all?

Discouraged by her failed task, the princess waited after school by the avenue for Mondo to arrive and take her home. She felt thankful for a quiet transport with few questions asked.

The week's end meant lessons were over for two days, giving her great relief. What should she do about the next quarter-moon's turn? Staying at the apartment appealed to her. Besides, who needed lessons when the entire world came into the Dovers' living chamber via a looking glass with moving pictures?

As Mondo's carriage headed down the last avenue toward the apartment, the enormity of Quinn's plan made her breath shallow.

Am I actually contemplating not returning home? Am I, the Royal Princess of the Kingdom of Mandria, willing to give up my throne to remain in this world? Nevermore to be a princess?

Princess Nevermore.

Quinn glanced at Mondo, wondering how shocked he'd be if she blurted out her idea. Her inner voice—which sounded an awful lot like Ameka—argued against her plan: *If you stay, you shall never become queen.*

Does it matter? Quinn argued back. *Is that what I truly want? Adam made it sound so boring and tedious when I tried to explain it to him.*

"Queen Quinn" had always sounded funny to her anyway. "Princess Nevermore" sounded better, albeit even that title made her sad.

Arriving at the apartment, she wandered to Adam's chamber to rest and continue her musing. *If I abdicate my throne, who will be next in line?*

Ay, yes. Dagon, son of her father's sister. She adored Dagon. He was funny and charming. They'd practically grown up as brother and sister until his grandfather at Pendrog died. Dagon's father, heir to the lordship of Pendrog Manor in the Kingdom of Twickingham, immediately moved the family to Twick to assume his duties as Lord Ryswick.

Dagon would make a fine king for the people of Mandria. Besides, she'd always suspected he fancied Ameka and wondered if he would ever come to court her. Such a match would please the princess.

And her own match? Pulling Adam's quilt around her for warmth, she considered her future. When Adam finished his schooling, perhaps they could begin a new life together.

In Mandria, she was expected to marry at sixteen. Well, she would. She'd marry Adam. Then her worries about choosing one of the young noblemen, due to come courting, would be over.

Would the king approve of Adam Dover? A lad who did not come from nobility—yet whose family had a vague connection to Mandria?

Pain twinged her heart at the thought of the king choosing a match for her, then being trapped in a loveless marriage. Such had happened to other princesses before her, according to Ameka, and it sounded like a lonely existence.

Quinn could hear her tutor's voice again—this time with a warning: *A hasty decision is thrice regretted.*

"Oh, but you would love Adam; I know you would," she whispered to Ameka as she hugged Adam's pillow. "In my heart of hearts, I have chosen my prince."

After they married, she and Adam would have heirs— no, children. Plain Outer-Earth children, not a prince and princess.

Would her parents be proud of their ordinary grandchildren? Surely the king and queen would allow her family to visit Mandria and would welcome them. Their visits between the worlds might even open the pathway for more Mandrians to travel to Outer Earth—perhaps to barter in this world's marketplaces.

As she straightened the quilt, the princess wondered if the life conjured up in her imagination sounded perfect simply because it was of her own choosing. Ay, the thrill of making choices!

Now all she had to do to ensure that her fantasy came true was convince Adam to forgive and forget—then hope to the High Spirit that her chosen prince returned the attraction and affection she felt for him.

22

Mondo's Story

After all her decision-making, the princess dozed.
When she awoke, Mondo was gone, Adam still wasn't home, and Sarah had left a note saying she was off with friends to prepare for the evening's ball. The princess hoped the family was not staying away from their own home on her account.

With pleasant surprise, Quinn noticed that the irritation in her throat had faded. She wondered if the discomfort had been related to the dream about Cam, which sparked it, or if Mondo's medicine did indeed work as well as a wizard's potion.

Hunger led the princess to the kitchen. She fixed a light repast of bread and left-behind poultry—the first time in her life she'd prepared her own food. It made her feel quite independent.

As Quinn gave the last bite of her feast to Katze, who'd been pestering her, a tinkling melody began to play. This sound was now familiar to her since it occurred in the apartment routinely. However, someone had always been present to lift the silver object and respond. The princess was not sure how the contraption worked.

The melody continued to play. Quinn reached for the object and held it to her ear the way she'd seen others do. "H–hello?"

"Hi."

Quinn was startled. First, because a voice talked back to her, and second, because the voice belonged to Zack.

"Yes?"

"How are you?" he asked in a pleasant tone.

She paused, not trusting his friendly manner. "I am well, thank you."

"I'll pick you up at seven."

She waited for him to tag on a sarcastic remark.

"Well, that's all. See you later."

Something clicked in her ear, then buzzed. Quinn set the object back on its shelf, wondering at the pleasant change in Zack.

Adam had told her the lad was decent until he started drinking. Almost every time she'd been near him, he smelled of spirits.

Quinn heard the front door open. She ran to greet Adam, but it was Mondo, carrying her Mandrian gown in a see-through wrapper.

"Adam said you'd be wearing this to the Halloween

dance. I noticed it was wrinkled and torn, so I had it cleaned and mended for you."A smile lit his face. "The owner of the laundry said your gown was made from the finest silk she'd ever seen. I told her the material was woven by Marnies from cocoons of the rare Mandrian silkworm."

The twinkle in Mondo's eyes told Quinn he'd enjoyed jesting about the dress with the shop's proprietress, even though his explanation was correct.

His mention of the wrinkled and torn gown drew her thoughts back to the moment Cam materialized in Melikar's chamber, causing her to tumble onto the cobblestone floor. Had it happened mere days ago?

Her heart ached with homesickness as well as pleasure that Mondo had taken care of her gown. She hugged him, practicing the Outer-Earth tradition she liked best.

Her actions surprised him. "You'd better get ready," he said, handing her the gown. "I want to see how you look before Adam arrives and whisks you away."

Quinn did not have the heart to tell him she was not attending the ball with his grandson. It would be hard to explain. Yet, after all of Mondo's cryptic words, it might please him if she were not in Adam's company.

Taking the gown, she hurried to change. Minutes later, she was transformed from an Outer-Earth maiden back into a Mandrian princess. She looked almost the same as when she arrived in this world, except her skin was no longer pale, her hair fell loose, and her eyelashes were dark and curled.

This reflection in the looking glass was the one most familiar to her—except for the canvas shoes. Kicking them off, she hunted until she found her jeweled Mandrian slippers. Katze had batted them under the bed.

After putting the cosmetics into the pocket of her gown and brushing tangles from her hair, Quinn found Mondo waiting in the living chamber.

He greeted her with an approving smile and bowed, as was the custom beneath the river. "You look beautiful, Quinn. Like a real Mandrian princess."

His attention embarrassed her. How did he know what a Mandrian princess looked like? "Can you braid my hair?" she asked.

Dividing her hair into three fat sections, Mondo clumsily patterned the lengths into one long braid, securing it with a band from the rolled parchment he spread out on the table every morning to read.

"Quinn," he began calmly as his fingers looped the band, "I think it's time for you to return to Mandria."

The casual comment shivered a chill through her. She twisted to face him. "But I have decided to remain in this world."

Immediately gathering her skirts, she departed from the chamber in haste, because she knew Mondo would protest, and she did not wish to hear his reasons.

"Wait," he said.

The princess did not turn back. Later, she would explain it all to Mondo—her plan to be part of both worlds, to return to Mandria with Adam for visits with her family. It all sounded reasonable; she'd convince Mondo to see it her way.

"Quinn!"

The tone of Mondo's voice stopped her. A youth could not defy an elder. As she trudged back, he motioned for her to sit.

Pulling her braid out of the way, she settled stiffly onto the cushions. Curiosity and reluctance battled inside of her.

"You cannot stay here," Mondo said. "You cannot be Adam's companion or anything else. You must forget him."

Quinn's spirit rebelled at every word. "You are trying to pretend Adam does not care for me, but honestly, he does."

Saying it out loud made it true; her heart said so. She gazed at Mondo through tear-blurred eyes. "You cannot keep us apart."

The boldness of her statement shocked her. Defying an elder came dangerously close to breaking a Mandrian truth. Taking a deep breath, Quinn begged the High Spirit to forgive her.

"Sire," she began, swallowing hard and forcing a steady voice, "why do you wish to keep me from Adam?"

Sighing, the old man sank to the cushions beside her. "I guess I'll have to tell you the truth."

He met her gaze. "I've never told anyone my secret,

but I don't know how else to make you understand. You are Mandrian. You don't belong in this world. You belong beneath the river."

"But I fit in perfectly," she argued, dabbing at her tears. "It has not been a problem at all." The lie stopped her. "Well, not much of a problem," she added. "Adam knows I am different. He does not care." At least she hoped her words were true.

"There's more to it than that, child."

Quinn glanced at him. He was beginning to sound a whole lot like Melikar. Grief shadowed his pool-colored eyes, making her forget her own troubles.

Mondo squeezed her hand with a fatherly tenderness. "I, too, am Mandrian. Born and schooled beneath the river. I come from a wealthy family of nobility, and I don't belong in this world any more than you do. It was a mistake for me to come and stay."

Mondo's words startled her, yet deep inside, she'd suspected he was Mandrian.

"What is so terrible about remaining in this world?" she asked.

"I'll tell you," he answered, watching her face as if he needed her to acknowledge the seriousness of his words. "When I was a few years past your age, I visited Melikar's chamber to entertain myself, the same way you do. I wanted to help him and learn from him—even become his apprentice. One of my aunts possessed the gift of Sight," he added, "so enchantment was a small part of my heritage."

Quinn's thoughts flashed to Cam. The apprentice with no family or history. As long as she'd known him, he'd lived with Melikar. Surely enchantment was part of his heritage, too.

"Just like you," Mondo continued, "I was fascinated with the wishing pool and those who came to make wishes." As he paused, his hands began to tremble.

"One day, a beautiful maiden came to the pool. I was captivated by her. She was as fragile as a wood nymph, with dark eyes and hair the color of coal from the Marnies' mine. Her hair was as long as the tresses of Mandrian maidens, too. She looked so wistful and . . . and lovely."

Quinn tried to be patient while Mondo lost himself in memories, but she was dying to hear the rest of the story. He seemed to have forgotten her presence until she lightly touched his arm.

He shuddered, coming out of his trance. "I'm sorry. It's been so long since I've allowed myself to recall this. After the first time I saw the maiden, she came often to the wishing pool."

Mondo turned away so Quinn could not see his face. "I fell hopelessly in love with her. I became obsessed with the very thought of her; with seeing her there above the pool.

"I wanted desperately to meet her, but Melikar wouldn't hear of it. I pleaded with him. He, alone, possessed the power to arrange a meeting. I promised, if he sent me to this world, I would bring the maiden back to

Mandria and make her my wife."

The princess listened, wide-eyed, to Mondo's astounding story.

"After much badgering on my part, Melikar finally gave in—on the condition that I return within hours, bringing the maiden, so she could preview what her life would be like in Mandria—a privileged life as the Lady of Kilmory Manor."

Quinn blinked at the familiar name. She knew of Kilmory Manor and of Lord and Lady Dover, now deceased. They must have been Mondo's parents. "You come from the Dovers of Kilmory?" she asked, amazed at how deeply his story reached into her world.

He nodded in a thoughtful way that told her he knew his parents were no longer living.

"Go on," she urged.

"Once Melikar finally agreed to send me, I dearly hoped the lovely lass would listen to my story and agree to travel back with me—not to stay at first, but just to visit the underground world. Likewise, I hoped the attraction between us was mutual and that she might wish to know me better."

The princess recalled how quickly she and Adam were drawn to each other, so she knew that instant attraction was certainly possible.

"The wizard made me pledge that the decision to remain in Mandria rested solely with the maiden," Mondo continued. "If, after seeing the underground world, she declined my proposal, I promised Melikar that both my heart and my mind would let her go. The wizard had the power to bring her here, then send her home without any lingering memories of Mandria or me."

Mondo's voice wavered from emotion. "I was ecstatic—convinced that once I showed her the world below the river and how wonderful life at Kilmory could be, she'd fall in love with it—and with me—and would never want to leave.

"I could hardly wait for the next morning. Melikar planned to cast the travel spell early, so I'd be waiting when the maiden arrived at the pool. I did not want to frighten her by suddenly appearing on the footbridge in odd garments and professing my love."

The princess nodded, remembering how relieved she'd felt that the area surrounding the wishing pool had been deserted the moment she materialized on the footbridge.

"Once the spell was cast, and I arrived in this world," Mondo continued, "I was beside myself, waiting to spot the maiden coming down the path toward the pool."

The old man's face changed.

"Mondo, what is it?"

His hands resumed their trembling. "She never came. I—I was frantic. Melikar's spell allowed me to remain above the river for only a short time. I adored the maiden too much to return without her, and I doubted the wizard would give me a second try."

Quinn took hold of Mondo's hands to steady them.

"In spite of Melikar's warning not to leave the pool, I followed the path through the forest and found the maiden working at a fairground—which is now Wonder-Land, the amusement park. That's why she came to the pool so often.

"I suppose it was better that we met at the fair under more normal circumstances. We liked each other instantly, just as I knew we would. Although she was curious about my strange clothes, she believed I was simply one of many young men who'd come to the fair that day.

"Up close, she was even more beautiful. Her name was beautiful, too. Hannah. I invited her to walk with me, so I could explain who I was and tell her of my plan—including Melikar's request that we return at once. But she insisted that I travel with her into the city instead. Her friends were having something she called a 'social,' and she wanted me to attend it with her."

Mondo gave a sad laugh. "Watching you on your first day here brought back all those memories of seeing the city for the first time. What a shock this world is to a Mandrian."

Sorrow tinged his face. "Of course, everything looked completely different in those days." He took a deep breath, then continued. "I knew I needed to reveal my true identity to Hannah, as I instructed you to tell Adam and Sarah the truth. I found it important to have an ally in this world.

"On the way to the social—at which we never

arrived—I told Hannah my story. She didn't believe it, of course, but when I tried to convince her to return to the pool with me simply to visit my homeland, she declined. I—I never considered the possibility of her *not* going back with me. But later, in retrospect, I completely understood why she refused. As I would soon learn, leaving one's home and family without saying why or good-bye is an enormous decision, fraught with emotion and guilt and regrets."

The princess knew his words were meant to be taken to heart with great seriousness since she was facing the same decision.

"Once Hannah made her choice, I was devastated. After all the intense emotions, I couldn't bear to return to Mandria alone. Now that I was finally in her glowing presence, leaving Hannah seemed impossible. Besides, she very much wanted me to stay.

"I was sure I'd enraged Melikar by not keeping my promise, but after the spell wore off, it was too late to return. The wizard might have been able to recast a travel spell, but by that time, I knew that I did not want to leave.

"Hannah took me to her brother's house. He lived alone, so I stayed with him and found employment carving wood and making cabinets. Working with wood had been my hobby in Mandria, learned from a old Marnie named Jol."

Mondo paused, as if rearranging memories in his mind. "In a few months, Hannah and I married and moved into our own home." His voice broke. "I never thought such happiness could be allowed one man. Hannah and I were deeply in love. Many years later, we had a son."

He buried his head in his hands.

Tears streamed down Quinn's face. "See? You wouldn't have given up Hannah for anything in the world. That's how I feel about Adam, and—"

"No!" Mondo jerked his hands away from his face. "My story is not yet finished. There's more—more that Melikar warned me about." His voice dropped to a shaky whisper. "But I was too taken with Hannah to listen."

Quinn could barely breathe, waiting for what was to come.

23

The Mandrian Secret

Dusk fell, leaving the room in shadows, yet neither the princess nor Mondo moved to turn on a light.

After all he's confessed, Quinn thought, *what more can he possibly say?*

Mondo seemed to be searching for strength to finish his story, so Quinn tried to help. "Sire, I know Hannah died. Adam and Sarah told me. They said you went away, and their father did not know where you'd gone."

"I never knew Adam and Sarah's father."

"But you must have. He was your son."

"No, child, he wasn't. And Hannah is not Adam and Sarah's grandmother."

Quinn watched his face, waiting for him to correct his obvious mistake, but he remained quiet. "Why did they tell me this?" she asked.

"It's what they've been told."

The princess tried to sort out what he was saying. "I do not understand."

Mondo tilted his head sideways to look at her. "Adam and Sarah's grandmother was Hannah's great-great-granddaughter."

Quinn did not want to appear rude, but it seemed the old man had lost his good sense. "That is impossible."

"I know it's hard to believe. Melikar warned me of the time difference between the worlds, but I was too young and foolish to be concerned with it." Mondo took her hand. "Don't you see? The time difference is why you cannot stay here with Adam."

"Why would it matter?"

Dropping her hand, he leaned back on the cushion and focused on the ceiling as though he were deep in thought. "Let me explain. I was twenty-years-old when I met Hannah. She was eighteen. One year in Mandria is more than three years in this world. Although Hannah was younger when we met, she soon grew older. She aged while I remained young."

Mondo stopped to remember. "When our son was born, the same thing happened. It sounds incredible, but my son and I were both thirty-six the same year. Yet, by the time I turned thirty-seven, he was almost forty. I was, and still am, aging in Mandrian years."

Quinn could not believe what she was hearing. "But Sarah and I are the same age."

"When Sarah was born, you were already ten years

old. In five Mandrian years, you'll be twenty, and Sarah will be thirty. Adam will be even older."

The mention of Adam's name made her realize what Mondo was trying to tell her. Still, even with this knowledge, how could she abandon her dream? "But, I thought you were *happy* with Hannah."

Quinn watched a tear roll down his wrinkled cheek. The love Mondo felt for his wife moved her, even though Hannah had died many, many years ago.

"Oh, yes, child. I was the happiest man in both worlds. Hannah was the love of my life. In my eyes, she never lost her beauty nor her youthfulness."

"How many years were you together?" Quinn's voice was barely a whisper.

"Sixty-two in this world. But only twenty Mandrian years. Not long by the standard I was used to. Hannah lived to be eighty. I was forty-one when she died."

Quinn's mind refused to comprehend the meaning of his words. "But it's wonderful that you had any time at all together. Why are you denying me the few years of happiness I could share with Adam?"

"You don't understand. When I said *happy*, I meant I was happy with *Hannah*. I was *miserable* with the kind of life we had to lead. We appeared to be a normal couple for only a few years. Then Hannah began to look older. As our son grew, others assumed he and I were brothers instead of father and son."

"Did you have other children?"

Mondo was quiet a long time, as if deciding how to

answer. "We chose to stop having children, lest they inherited the trait of aging in Mandrian years."

"How did you keep people from discovering your secret?" Quinn asked. Perhaps she'd need this information if she found herself in the same predicament.

"We moved frequently. At first, people discriminated against us because they believed Hannah had married a much younger man. It wasn't proper in those days. And poor Hannah. It broke her heart to hear our names mentioned in gossip. Then, a few years later, folks assumed she was my mother—which broke her heart even more.

"Finally, we found it easier to pretend we were mother and son to avoid being set apart as different. Then, rumors began about why I lived at home and never married. Whenever rumors became unbearable, we'd move again. Of course, our son suffered the discrimination, too."

Mondo tugged at his beard, lost in thought. "At that point, Hannah *wanted* to go to Mandria. In fact, she begged me to take her, thinking it would be her fountain of youth, and she'd remain young, like me. Unfortunately, it doesn't work that way. There, she'd still age in Outer-Earth years.

"Besides, I worried that the discrimination might be worse in the underground world since the caste one is born into rules all else. Even though Hannah was a nobleman's wife, she would still be considered an outsider. She'd never be accepted by the ladies of the court. I couldn't put her through the trauma of leaving one world to end her pain, only to find deeper pain in the other."

"What happened then?" Quinn's heart was shattering into pieces. Still, she wanted to know how the story ended.

"Eventually, people figured Hannah was my grandmother. We let them believe whatever they wanted. The strain was too difficult for our son, who, by then, appeared to be my father. He traveled west after the turn of the century and rarely kept in touch. I'm not sure he ever forgave me for what I put him and his mother through—merely by my staying young."

Mondo glanced at Quinn. "Regardless, I did keep track of my descendants over the years. Giving them all up would have been too painful. They never knew I was watching, but oftentimes a gift would arrive for a new baby or money would come when most needed, all from Great-Grandfather Dover—even though it may actually have been great-great-great-grandfather. So, they knew *of* me, yet never knew exactly where I was."

Mondo ran a shaky hand through his hair. "The hardest part of all, Quinn, was watching Hannah die." His voice broke as the tears came.

"When two people age together, one can help the other through each stage of life. But what could I offer my wife as she lay dying? Her body had worn out, yet mine was still strong. I know how much Hannah loved me, but I swear when I looked into her eyes on our last day together, I saw resentment. I saw a loving person who could no longer forgive me for being what I am. A Mandrian."

As the old man gave in to tears, so did Quinn. Putting her arms around him, they held each other, weeping freely.

Mondo pulled a handkerchief from his pocket and blotted Quinn's tears, then his own.

The princess had no desire to hear any more of his sadness, but when he was able to speak again, she let him finish.

"After I lost Hannah, I spent countless years wandering this world, cursing the High Spirit for not taking me at the same time."

"Why did *you* not return to Mandria?"

"I considered it, but I would have been discriminated against as well. I couldn't simply reappear in the kingdom after all those years and expect to resume my status as the rightful Lord of Kilmory Manor. When I disappeared, I'm sure everyone believed I'd gone to the world of spirits."

He smiled. "Besides, how does one explain a tanned face and premature wrinkles to a Mandrian? I would have been considered an oddity in my homeland."

Mondo tucked his handkerchief into a pocket. "Another reason I chose not to return was simply because I'd grown accustomed to life here. Once you've experienced the pleasure of a rainstorm, had the breeze tousle your hair, felt the sun warm your face, or inhaled the wonderful scents of the forest, it's quite a difficult decision to leave it all behind."

His Mandrian eyes twinkled for a second as he added. "Did I mention giving up television and cars, computers and cell phones? Returning to Mandria would be like going back in time."

Quinn commiserated with his dilemma. Could one who'd sampled pizza be content again with porridge?

Mondo grew serious again. "Now I have Adam and Sarah to watch over, which is the best reason of all for remaining in a world I never belonged in."

Quinn nodded, yet one thing still bewildered her. "If your family never knew where you were," she asked, "how did you know to return for Adam and Sarah?"

"Melikar told me."

Quinn gasped. "Melikar can contact you?"

"His powers are strong, child. I can always tell when my thoughts are not my own. He made me aware of the plight of my—" Mondo squinted his eyes as he counted. "My great-great-great-grandchildren—give or take a few greats."

Quinn still had difficulty believing it.

"He also told me of your arrival. It was no coincidence that we went to WonderLand Park that day. My purpose was to find you and take care of you for as long as you are on this side of the pool."

"But it all happened so fast. How did you—?"

"Melikar's magic reaches deep into this world. It's a Mandrian truth."

Mondo glanced at the timepiece on his wrist. "Are you ready to leave for the dance?" His question seemed ridiculously commonplace after the conversation they'd just shared, making the worries of the present tumble back into Quinn's mind.

"I suppose."

He caught her arm as she stood. "This truth I've told you must not leave this room." He lifted two fingers to his cheek, giving her the Sign of the Lorik.

"It will be our secret," she agreed, returning the sign.

Mondo clicked on the lights.

Quinn took a deep breath and straightened her gown, wondering if her makeup was smudged from wiping away tears.

As she turned to leave, Mondo added in a calm voice. "Now that you know the consequences, child, I expect you to do the right thing."

She nodded, not replying with her tongue, because her heart spoke a different answer. Wasn't a few years of happiness with her heart's choice worth more than the pain of living in a world without him?

Mondo had not swayed her decision.

She fully intended to remain in Adam's world.

24

Going to the

Ball

$\mathcal{T}$he unbelievable secret Mondo had entrusted to the princess was suffocating her. She had to get out of the apartment.

Bidding him good-bye, Quinn went out the door and sat on the front steps. Taking deep breaths of crisp evening air to calm herself, she cringed at what lay ahead.

The last thing she needed tonight was Zack.

Right now Quinn's heart ached for another young maiden who'd also been in love, only that maiden was born more than one hundred and fifty Outer-Earth years ago. Her heart also ached because Mondo expected her to say good-bye to Adam.

The princess arranged her billowing yards of skirts. Wearing Mandrian clothes again felt odd. Now *they* seemed uncomfortable.

A screeching sound caught her attention. Below her, on the avenue, a car recklessly careened to a stop.

Zack.

Quinn repressed an urge to dash back into the apartment and hide. In all fairness, she must uphold the wager the three of them had struck. It was an Outer-Earth truth. Or did such a truth exist?

She was the reward, and, as her station in life commanded, she would honor the challenge as did the lads, holding her head high until her obligation was fulfilled.

The princess waited, but Zack did not come up to fetch her.

Rising, she descended the stairs with hesitant feet. As she reached the avenue, Zack sprang from his carriage and gave her an approving look-over. "Let me guess," he said, scratching his head. "You're a princess, right?"

Quinn's heart faltered before she remembered that her gown was meant to be a costume.

"Where's your crown?" he teased. "We could make one for you out of tin foil."

The princess lifted her chin proudly and pretended to jest. "My crown is kept in a crystal case in the throne room of my castle to be worn only on royal occasions. It is carved of pure gold and set with seven precious gems."

"Oh." Zack seemed amused at her teasing wit. "That sure beats tin foil."

As they climbed into the carriage, Quinn examined his costume: leather pants, a vest with no shirt beneath it, a scarf tied around his neck, gloves with the fingers cut out, and boots.

His hair was slicked back on the sides. Dangling from one ear was a trinket like Sarah wore. Quinn had no idea what his costume was supposed to signify.

Before they could depart, another car screeched to a stop beside them. Zack spoke briefly to a lad who leaned out a window and handed him a carrier of bottles, then sped off.

"My friends," he explained, making his carriage surge forward. He flipped the top off one of the bottles, releasing the familiar aroma that often seemed to surround him. He took swigs of the liquid as he moved the carriage—a little too fast and reckless for Quinn's comfort.

When they arrived at school, Zack took long strides toward the entrance to the large chamber where scholars played sports. Quinn trotted to keep up with him.

Stepping through double doors, the princess stopped, eyes wide, forgetting about Zack. The chamber had become enchanted. The dimly lit room was filled with colored balls floating against the ceiling. Crinkly paper hung in streamers along the walls.

Loud music struck Quinn's ears, different from any music she'd ever heard. Costumed scholars moved in rhythm to the music. Its beat was so overpowering, the princess felt as if her heartbeat had changed to match the music's rhythm.

Zack steered her into a corner. He stood next to her for a moment, arms crossed, tapping his foot to the music, then gave her a sidelong glance. "Guess the fun's in winning—not in having. At least not until later."

While she was trying to interpret Zack's words, he added, "Gotta go see some friends. Stay here."

He disappeared through the crowd, leaving the princess alone, like a forgotten trophy.

She did not mind being left alone. The sights and music hypnotized her. Even the young folk seemed enchanted as they twirled about the dance floor in their lavish or funny or puzzling costumes. Most music in Mandria was soft and slow with deliberate steps to each ballroom pavane.

She wondered if these dances *had* deliberate steps. Everyone moved a bit wildly. It appeared to be great fun—albeit not proper behavior for a princess.

Quinn watched the crowd and searched for Adam. Would he come to the ball after what happened at the joust? Would he bring another maiden? Jealousy tickled her heart.

The music was so inviting, the princess could hardly stand still. She wanted to try the dance. If Adam were here, he'd show her how. *The least Zack can do is—*

"Hey!"

Roger, in his knight's costume, worked his way toward her. He held hands with a girl who looked beauti-ful in a short, fuzzy costume with floppy ears and a fluffy tail. Quinn remembered seeing a photo of her in Roger's car.

Quinn curtsied, even though in Mandria the lad would be required to bow before her. She held out one hand. "Sir Roger, I bid you good evening."

He returned the bow, kissing her hand. "Lady Quinn," he quipped. "This is Wendy. She has given me permission to dance with you."

The maiden slapped him playfully. "Go on. I'll get something to drink."

"I don't think they have carrot juice," Roger teased.

Wendy groaned, then pretended to hop toward the refreshment table.

Watching Roger and Wendy jest with each other made Quinn feel even worse about Adam's absence.

Roger grabbed her hand. "Come on. This is a great song."

Quinn followed, trying to catch up. "Wait," she called, raising her voice above the commotion. "I do not know how to dance this way."

He stopped beside two whirling monsters with shaggy heads. "You don't know how to dance?"

"No." *Not like this*, her mind added.

"Where in the world are you from?"

She started to say, "*Which* world?" but smiled instead, acting as though he were teasing.

"Doesn't matter; I'll teach you. All you have to do is feel the beat of the music, then move to it."

Young folk around them stared as Roger demonstrated while she stood still. Embarrassed, Quinn wished she could hide again behind the pig mask.

"Will you teach me the steps?"

"There *are* no steps." He grabbed her hands and

moved with her until she sensed his rhythm and moved on her own. Then he dropped her hands and spun around. "You're dancing, Princess!"

Quinn laughed, imitating the movements of maidens around her. It felt wonderful and free. She loved the loudness and the overflowing crowd of young folk all moving together, yet separately,

With the next song, she relaxed. Mr. French danced by with a maiden from homeroom. He looked a little silly, acting like a youth.

Then she caught sight of Zack dancing with a maiden dressed in a skimpy animal skin and tall leather boots. Why would Zack make a fuss over bringing her to the ball, then desert her for another?

In a few minutes, the music slowed. Couples stepped close, dancing with their arms around each other.

"Do you know how to slow dance?" Roger asked.

Unsure what "slow dance" meant, Quinn shook her head.

He placed her left hand on his shoulder and took her right hand in his. "Take small steps now, and follow my lead."

It was awkward at first, until she realized he was showing her which way to step by the way he moved her arm. Finally, a dance similar to ones in Mandria!

Once Quinn got the feel of it, she glanced around and was shocked at how close some of the couples were dancing. It was a sight she'd never seen beneath the river. She tried not to watch, but couldn't resist.

Roger fell silent as they danced. Was he never going to mention Adam unless she broached the topic? Her stomach knotted, waiting for him to say something. Finally she asked, "Have you seen Adam tonight?

He looked relieved, as if he'd been waiting for the question. "No, I came with Wendy. The last time I talked to him, he hadn't decided whether or not to come."

Roger hesitated. "It's none of my business, but Adam is my best friend, and he's really upset about losing the joust—especially since Zack cheated."

The princess nodded, taking the blame upon her heart.

"And he told me you guys aren't really cousins but wouldn't tell me why you started such a weird rumor. Anyway, he likes you a whole lot."

"Still?"

"Still." He squeezed her hand to make his point. "Zack is responsible for this mix-up, not you. Adam knows that. But he tends to let jealousy get the better of him."

"He's jealous of Zack?"

"Sure. Most guys are. Zack has a habit of stealing girlfriends."

"But Adam has nothing to worry about. I'd rather—"

"I'll take it from here," interrupted a slurred voice. Zack jerked Quinn's arm from Roger's shoulder.

Roger started to say something, then stopped. Giving her a sympathetic look, he headed back to Wendy.

Zack gruffly clutched the princess to him, forcing

her arms around his neck. "A bunch of my friends are driving out to WonderLand Park later. You and I are going, too. We need to have a long talk."

He stared down at her. "About this weird hobby of yours—playing magician or whatever you call it—well, I want to know how you do it."

Zack was almost smothering her against him. "Think what I could do with that kind of power." He said it more to himself than to her.

The song ended. Still, he continued to crush her.

When she pushed away, he let go, causing her to fall backward into another couple. The other lad caught the princess to keep her from falling. "Are you all right?" he asked.

"Yes, thank you," she said, straightening her gown.

The lad's dance partner was dressed in feathers with a beak protruding from her forehead. "I'm going to powder my nose," she said to Quinn. "Want to come?"

Zack offered his hand as another song began.

Eager to get away from him, yet not knowing where one went to powder one's nose or what one powdered it with, the princess eagerly agreed.

Ignoring Zack's outstretched hand, Quinn followed the bird-maiden off the dance floor.

25

The Breaking
of the Sign

~

"How'd you get Zack to invite you to the dance?" the feathered maiden asked as they wove their way through the crowd surrounding the dancers.

"I beg your pardon?" Quinn did not know what she was talking about

"I've been working on him for *weeks*, then *you* come along—you're new here, aren't you?" She paused, but didn't give Quinn time to answer. "And he goes and asks you. What did you say to make him—?"

Quinn didn't hear the rest of the question because a brown-dappled horse bumped into them. Off came the horse's head to reveal one of the lads Quinn had seen chasing the ball in the meadow behind the school.

"Mi–chael!" the maiden cried, turning away from Quinn and giving him her full attention.

The princess waited, but the bird-maiden and horse-lad were busy flirting and teasing. She feared Zack might come looking for her, so she retreated to the girls' room, thankful for a place to hide.

She wasn't alone.

Among a group of maidens stood Sarah, positioned in front of the looking-glass, arranging her hair. She wore a shredded black gown over black jeans.

As the maiden set a pointed hat on top of her head, Quinn worried over whether to leave or attempt to make amends. Before she could do either, Sarah noticed her.

"Hey," she said softly. "I need to talk to you."

The friendliness in Sarah's voice was unexpected. The princess moved closer, out of earshot of the others, eager to hear what the maiden had to say. If anyone knew Adam's whereabouts, it would be his sister.

"I want to thank you," Sarah said.

This was not what the princess expected to hear. "Thank me? For what?"

"Well, this is hard to explain, but—" Sarah held out one hand, displaying a thin silver ring with a green stone in the center. "It's from Scott. It means he's my boyfriend."

The princess dutifully admired the ring.

"Oops," Sarah added. "You probably don't know what 'boyfriend' means. Um, it means we're seeing only each other."

The princess was not sure how two people could see only each other and not everyone else, but she smiled and said, "I'm happy for you, Sarah, but what does it have to do with me?"

Sarah gawked at her as though the point she was trying to make was obvious. "If you hadn't come along and taken away Zack's attention, I never would have given Scott a chance." Facing the looking-glass, she dotted color onto her lips. "I was mad at you at first, but Scott was so understanding and nice. Getting to know him made me realize how dumb I've been for letting Zack treat me so horribly."

Quinn was pleased that the uncomfortable situation had ultimately benefited the maiden.

"So," Sarah finished, giving her a hug, "you brought Scott and me together. Thank you, thank you. And I'm sorry I didn't help you at school the way I promised. Can we start over?"

Quinn agreed, pleased by Sarah's apology even though she no longer needed the maiden's help. *Now is probably not the best time to inform her of my decision to stop taking lessons.*

"I'm really glad you and my brother like each other," Sarah added. "I'm sure, after tonight, you two can patch things up."

The princess felt as if a great burden had been lifted from her heart. "I shall always value your friendship—just like a sister's." She gave Sarah the Sign of the Lorik.

Sarah gave a weak, "Oh, no," as her face drained of color. She started to return the sign, then stopped, curling her fingers into a fist and lowering her hand. "Oh,

Quinn, I've done something terrible."

The princess waited, but the maiden didn't offer an explanation. "Go on," she said, urging Sarah to continue.

"Um . . . please . . . stay away from Zack."

"Pardon? How can I stay away from him? He won my presence in the joust, and I must honor the outcome."

"Listen to me," the maiden implored in a shaky whisper. "Zack knows."

A chill iced through the princess. "He knows *what*?" Afraid to hear Sarah's answer, she added, "You mean, he knows of Mandria?"

The door burst open and a noisy group of laughing maidens tripped into the chamber.

Sarah's silence was answer enough. Quinn yanked her into a corner of the room so no one would hear. "You told Zack my secret?"

Sarah squirmed, absently rearranging her dress. "I didn't tell him *all* of it. He just kept *bugging* me about you. He knows there's something different about you; I don't know how he suspected it."

Quinn took a deep breath to quell her anger. She'd known Sarah was upset—but never would have believed the maiden might break the Lorik sign. Beneath the river, a broken sign was unforgivable. It was a Mandrian truth.

"I never mentioned the Kingdom of Mandria," Sarah said in a trembly voice. "I just hinted that you . . . you have a special power."

The princess recalled Zack's words: *Think what I*

could do with that kind of power.

Sarah began to cry.

"It's all right." Quinn patted her shoulder like Jalla used to pat her as a child. It certainly was *not* all right, but what else could she say?

The other maidens stopped talking to stare at them in curiosity.

Quinn dropped her voice to a whisper. "I'm glad you did not speak to him of Mandria. If he questions my power, I shall pretend I do not know what he's talking about." A ghastly thought struck her. "You did not tell him about the *ring*, did you?"

Sarah wiped her eyes on a hand-drying cloth. "I–I don't know. I can't remember."

Quinn bit her lip to keep from saying more. It was not her place to reprimand the maiden. A sign of true royal blood was the ability to pardon one who has harmed you—a truth the princess always found difficult.

"Please forgive me," Sarah whispered.

This new burden suffocated the princess even more than Mondo's confession. The walls of the chamber began to close in. She needed to go outside to be alone and to calm her annoyance with the lass.

"It is forgotten," Quinn lied, trying in vain to smile. "I'm truly happy for you and Scott."

Sarah looked immensely relieved. "We're going out to WonderLand Park later. Want to come?"

The remembrance of Zack's command made her head throb. "I shall be going to the park as well. Perhaps I'll see you there."

Sarah hugged her one last time. "You look fab tonight," she said, raising her voice so the other maidens could hear. "Just like a real princess."

Their eyes locked in the looking-glass—Sarah's bright with renewed enthusiasm, and Quinn's dark with the threat of an ancient fear.

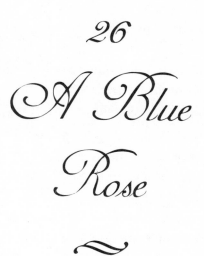

26

A Blue Rose

Panic rose in Quinn's chest as she hurried from the girls' room.

Veering the opposite direction from the dancers, she disappeared into a darkened corridor.

Couples, scattered here and there, talked intimately. Some were kissing. Quinn tried not to look, but could not help herself. Beneath the river, a lad stealing a kiss in public was scandalous.

Hurrying past, Quinn came to the double doors at the end of the corridor and burst outside. Her gown offered little protection from the brisk night air. Hugging herself to keep from shivering, she longed for the warmth of a hooded traveling cape.

The princess was relieved to be alone with her worries. She leaned against a brick wall, lit by an overhanging lamp, to ponder Sarah's words.

Zack.

Toads and mugwort, how the lad has messed up my enjoyment of this world.

Yet, Quinn knew she could handle him. She would simply deny anything he might accuse her of—including the possession of a magic ring.

Perhaps a more urgent worry was Mondo's story. Why had he sworn her to secrecy? Revealing this newest Mandrian truth to Adam seemed crucial, yet she'd pledged Mondo the Lorik sign not to tell.

A door creaked open.

Quinn stiffened. She hoped those intruding on her privacy were merely an enamored couple, seeking to be alone. Instead, a single dark figure appeared.

"Quinn?" came a voice from the shadows.

"Adam?"

Emotions tumbled through the princess at the sound of his voice.

He stepped into the shaft of light and gazed at her for a long moment before scooping her into his arms.

"I am sorry," she whispered, hugging him tightly, as if it would bond their worlds together.

"*I'm* the one who should be apologizing," he told her, "for acting like a jealous idiot. I've missed you."

Stepping back, Adam pulled a single flower from inside his jacket. "It's a blue rose. Blue to match your gown—and the mood I've been in without you. I want you to wear it in your hair tonight." He threaded the flower stem between the loops of her braid.

"After this annoying night is over," he added, "will you consider going out with me—and no one else?"

"Does that mean you'll be my boyfriend?" Quinn asked, using the words she'd heard others use.

Adam laughed. "Has someone taken over my tutoring job?"

"Sarah explained it to me."

"Oh, good. Are you two friends again?"

"We mended our misunderstanding."

"I'm glad," he whispered. Growing serious, he studied her face in the lamplight. "Princess, I've thought about you constantly. I really want you to stay in my world."

Quinn's fears jumbled together, like pieces of an all-black puzzle. His words were precisely the ones she'd longed to hear, yet now that he'd said them, she did not know how to respond. Mondo's story and Sarah's confession prevented her from relaxing and being present in this time and place with Adam.

"I cannot go to lessons anymore," she told him for lack of a better answer. "The headmaster is suspicious."

"No problem. We'll get you a tutor—a *real* one. And you can live with us as long as you'd like. The college I plan to attend is nearby; I can come home on weekends. Maybe I can convince you to join me there."

"College?"

"Oh, jeez, you keep me on my toes. Um . . ." He paused, squinting at the dark sky to think. "Going to

college is like becoming an apprentice. Here, your
friend Cam would attend college to become a wizard—
if it were possible. That would be his career."

"Career?"

"Yeah. What you do with your life—what you want
to be."

"You mean, you *choose* what you want to be?"

"Well, of course."

Quinn put one hand to her head, feeling sure it was
going to burst if she received any more incredible news
tonight. She'd never considered what she *wanted* to be.
She was a princess. Her life didn't offer choices.

Part of her felt pleased to know Adam had made
plans that included her—yet he had not mentioned marriage. Not marrying in her youth—or being betrothed—
was an appalling disgrace for a Mandrian maiden.

Quinn shifted, turning away, embarrassed at being
the one to bring up such a topic. It was not her accepted
role. "Pray tell, when do people in your world marry?"

Adam gave a hearty laugh.

She faced him as he leaned against the wall, wondering at his reaction, unsure of what it meant.

"I forgot," he began. "Mandrian princesses are
expected to marry at sixteen. Here, that's considered way
too young."

"There's nothing *wrong* with our ways," Quinn told
him, raising her chin with pride. "I've even thought of
you as a possible choice."

"You have?" His voice softened as he brushed stray

wisps of hair from her forehead. "I've thought of you as a possible choice, too."

She did not know whether to feel pleased or indignant. "Your plans for the future include me, but not . . ." Feeling mortified by the conversation, she paused, unable to bring herself to say it.

"Oh, Princess." In the shadowed light, Adam's loving gaze pierced her to the spirit. He drew her from the shadows to better see her face. "I fell in love with you the moment you appeared on the bus at WonderLand Park and offered me your hand."

Pulling her close, he gave her a tender kiss.

At that moment, nothing else in either world mattered, except his lips gently touching hers.

"There's a whole other world on this side of the wishing pool," he told her. "Let me show you what it has to offer. After that, you'll be ready for anything, and the *last* thing you might want is to marry me—or to marry at all."

"You mean *not* marrying isn't a disgrace?"

Quinn shivered, half from the bitter air and half from Adam's nearness. Or was it from all he was telling her?

He laughed at her amazed response. "Boy, have *you* got a lot to learn. We've plenty of time for weddings."

Plenty of time is *not* what she had in Mandria.

"You're shivering," he said with concern. "Take my jacket."

Quinn expected Adam to be wearing the knight's costume beneath his outer garment. How disappointing to see him dressed in regular clothes.

She obliged Adam by putting on his jacket, gratefully shoving her cold hands into the deep pockets for warmth. Closing her eyes, she felt her head swim with all the hopeful things they had talked about. Yet the burden of Mondo's secret remained, like a hidden weight, tugging at her heart and ruining her joy.

"I would love to stay in your world—truly I would. But there is something important you must know before you make future plans." Quinn paused, wondering how to tell him without breaking the Lorik sign. Perhaps she could implore Mondo to reveal the truth to Adam. He needed to know. And it was Mondo's secret to tell, not hers.

The lad pulled her close. "Nothing you could possibly tell me will change my mind about you." He smiled endearingly. "So, what is it, Princess? What is this 'something important' you must tell me?"

Before she could answer, the door leading from school flew open.

Coldness penetrated Quinn's heart as Zack burst from the shadows, striding toward them with angry steps.

27

Return to WonderLand

~

The sight of Zack caused Quinn's heart to topple in on itself. Withdrawing her arms from Adam's neck, she stepped away, then wondered why she had bothered to hide her true feelings from Zack.

"Hey," the lad said. "Excuse me for interrupting." His words were polite, but his tone sounded derisive.

Quinn focused on the lad's face in the faint light. She recalled the phone call and how polite he'd sounded. Adam had commented about Zack's changing personality. She did not care to be with someone when she did not know how he was going to react—nice or nasty.

"Since you're *my* date for the evening," Zack said, "it's time to go. My friends are ready to leave for WonderLand Park." He gave Adam a sidelong glance, neither friendly nor malicious. "I'll wait for you inside."

Zack sauntered back toward the school, taking his time as though he wanted them to be distracted by his presence.

The princess was afraid to meet Adam's eyes. "Farewell, for now," she told him, confused by Zack's cryptic behavior.

Adam scowled at the retreating form.

"Are you jealous again?" she teased.

"You're way too good for him," Adam said. "You deserve the best. You deserve me."

They held onto each other, touching foreheads. The princess was reluctant to let go of the moment and knew that Adam felt the same way.

"You know, you don't really have to leave with him," Adam finally whispered.

"Oh, but I do. I cannot deny my obligation any more than you could deny the challenge to joust."

"Ah, the honorable princess and her Mandrian truths."

He let go of her and stepped away. "Okay, then. I hate to see you go off with him. I don't trust the guy."

Adam crossed his arms as if holding back his emotions. "Please be careful. I'm trying to understand why you have to go through with this—this cultural commitment that's so different from how we act in our world." He sighed. "Just know that I'll be waiting at home for you." He reached one hand to stroke her cheek the way he did the first day. "Remember, Quinn of Mandria, I adore you."

His tenderness made her heart melt like butter in a hot cauldron. "At home, we say, 'My heart embraces you.'"

"My heart embraces you," he repeated. "I like that." He raised two fingers to form the Sign of the Lorik. "Till later."

"Till later," she agreed, returning the sign.

The princess walked briskly along the edge of the building and entered the school. Already, she longed for the evening's end, especially since she knew Adam would be waiting for her at the apartment. They would hug and laugh over the traumatic day, then leave it behind them.

And from that point forward, their lives together would begin. *Joy!* The princess's heart filled with elation at the thought of starting a new journey down a path of her own choosing.

The sight of Zack waiting in the corridor quickly doused the feelings of joy.

"Thought you'd disappeared on me," he said, watching her face for a reaction.

Quinn caught the double meaning of his words but did not comment.

Zack shrugged as if he didn't expect an answer, then whipped around and headed down the corridor.

The princess followed, wondering why the lad always walked ahead of her instead of by her side.

As they re-entered the main chamber, the dim atmosphere, music, and strange assortment of weird creatures startled Quinn as much as they had the first time she'd stepped into the room.

Zack strode across the floor without stopping. Quinn hurried to keep up, dodging dancers. A lad she did not know stepped in front of her to block her path. He was dressed as a walrus with two sharp tusks hanging almost to the floor. She'd read stories about such creatures in the oceans of Outer Earth.

The lad did not speak. He simply handed her one of the colored balls tied with a string, then danced away. Fascinated, she let go of the string so she could grasp the red sphere. The ball rose from her grasp and floated to the ceiling. "Magic," she whispered, watching the ball bob its way into place beside others.

As she followed Zack, her eyes met Mr. French's. He pointed at her and frowned. She waved, knowing how confused the man would be next week when she did not come to lessons at all.

Once outside, Quinn realized she was still wearing Adam's jacket. Should she ask Zack to wait while she returned it? On second thought, maybe she'd be glad to have its warmth at WonderLand Park. Besides, being surrounded with something of Adam's might give her strength to go through with her unpleasant obligation.

When they got into Zack's carriage, he immediately reached behind the seat to fetch a bottle. "Want one?" he asked, twisting off the cap.

"No, thank you," Quinn replied. She hated to see him drinking now that she knew it made him act like a

Marnie who'd inhaled too much vapor from gold ore tailings in the mines.

They rode in silence. Quinn watched the sights of the city flash by and wished it were daylight so she could see everything better. Outlines of tall buildings made of looking-glass reflected the light of a full moon. Full moon.

The princess shuddered. Sometimes in Mandria during this phase of the moon that shone above the outside world, strange creatures appeared, usually in the outlying tunnels that connected the kingdoms. Quinn was never allowed to tarry outside of castle walls on those nights. She wondered if a full moon caused eerie things to happen in this world, too.

Beyond the bright moon lay the night sky. And stars.

How many were there? Quinn could not take it all in. As long as she might live in this world, she would never tire of gazing at the vastness of its heavens.

Someday in the future, when she returned to visit Mandria, she'd tell them of Outer-Earth magic: light without candles, talking to someone far away through an object as small as one's hand, moving pictures on a looking-glass. What a stir these things would cause in the underground kingdoms.

Suddenly Zack swerved the carriage to avoid hitting one in the next lane. Quinn held onto the seat with both hands, bracing her feet against the sloped floor. The sensation of traveling at great speed frightened her. The lad kept weaving between cars. He emptied the bottle, tossed it onto the seat behind them, and reached for another. Quinn worried that the drinking of spirits while steering a carriage might not be a good practice.

Finally, the carriage turned into a large field where many carriages were parked. In the distance, Quinn could see the giant arch aglow with twinkling colors:

WELCOME TO WONDERLAND PARK

How odd to return to the park wearing my Mandrian gown.

Zack brought the carriage to a stop and got out. He did not open the door for the princess the way Mondo did, so she got out on her own and waited while he took off the leather vest, put on the tunic with the large numeral on the front, then pulled the vest back on.

They entered the park. Multi-colored lights sparkled in the night. Noisy crowds gathered around the same whirring machines that had scared the princess so much when she first arrived. People here were dressed in costume, as well. In fact, Quinn spotted two other "princesses" in the area. At least she did not have to worry about blending in this time.

Zack hurried her through the crowd, past vendors selling treats, fountains spraying colored water into the air in time to music, and a stage featuring a baker's dozen young folk, singing and dancing.

The princess wanted to tarry at every attraction and booth, but Zack wouldn't stop. *He must be late for the meeting with his friends,* Quinn thought, following him to a shadowed corner near the edge of the forest. Beyond them, a winding path disappeared into the dark trees. Next to the path was a sign that read:

To The Wishing Pool

"Where are your friends?" Quinn asked, not wanting to be alone with him—especially if he planned on heading down the path in the dark.

"They're not here." Zack took a brisk swig from a bottle he'd hidden in his jacket.

"But you said—"

"I lied."

Nearby, a park servant urged people off the footpath so he could shut the gate. "Closing for the night in five minutes," he told everyone.

A biting numbness made Quinn wrap Adam's jacket tightly around herself. Of course, the knave would lie to her. His confession did not surprise her.

"Why did you bring me here?" she demanded.

"There's something you have that I want."

His leering grin chilled Quinn to her inner spirit.

The lad grabbed the sleeve of Adam's jacket and yanked the princess away from the park servant and the people exiting the path. "You know how to make things happen," he told her. "You have some sort of . . . of power."

"No, I—"

"Don't deny it. I've seen you do things. More than once. I even waited for you to use the power during the joust—but you didn't."

He bent to her eye level. "Why *didn't* you?" His eyes were red and a little out of focus. "You had the power to make Dover win."

The princess met his gaze. "I do not know what you're talking about."

"Don't lie to me. I know about the ring."

Shock bolted through her. Sarah *had* told him.

The thought of Zack gaining control of the magic ring choked the living breath from her.

He grinned, glancing around and acting as though they were having a normal conversation. "No one will mess with me," he told her. "I'll zap them, and they'll leave me alone." He raised his bottle high in the air as if toasting himself. "I'll have all the money I want. I'll have *anything* I want."

Devil dust! Quinn swore, begging the High Spirit to forgive her.

The wood nymph's story sprang to mind. The earth had once been filled with magic—until evil men stole the power from enchanted creatures for their own wicked intentions.

It was happening all over again. The lad wanted her magic for his evil purposes.

"Show it to me," Zack hissed, grabbing her by the shoulders.

Quinn twisted away from him, vowing to go to her grave before allowing the knave to take the ring. He held her tight by one arm.

Use the ring now, her mind warned. *Stop him with the magic.*

No, she argued. *Then he will l know I possess the power. He'll be after me all the time. I'll never be safe from him.*

Her mind reeled, searching for a way out. She could *not* let this happen. *I must get away from him without using the magic.*

Zack was so much bigger that he could take the ring as easily as Katze had taken scraps of poultry from her earlier.

"Give it to me now," he demanded. "And I'll take you home."

Frantically, the princess worked at the ring with her thumb until it slipped off her finger and dropped deep into the pocket of Adam's jacket.

Now what?

Sudden voices broke through the trees as the final hikers emerged from the footpath. Zack let go of her, acting as if nothing was amiss. He stepped away while the small crowd passed.

Sarah and Scott exited the path, hand in hand.

"Quinn!" Sarah cried, waving. "Are you having a good time?" She ignored Zack, who, in turn, ignored her.

"Ay—" Quinn's mind went blank. What could she say to alert Sarah to the danger? "I—"

"Yeah, we're having a great time." Zack waved the two off. "See ya around."

"Well, bye," Sarah called as she passed.

"Wait!" the princess hollered as she slipped off the jacket. "Adam must be freezing without this. Would you give it to him for me?"

"Sure." Sarah grabbed the jacket, then ran to catch up with Scott.

Quinn let her breath out slowly. Now the ring was safe. After tonight, she'd never dare wear it again. She'd find a good hiding place in the apartment to make sure the source of the magic remained safe.

Now that Zack would never possess the ring, there was nothing left to fear. All she had to do was fulfill her obligation by returning to the city with him. Then this horrible night would be over, and she could get on with the rest of her life. A life that did not include Zack.

"I have kept my promise to attend the ball with you," the princess said. "We are finished with the evening's celebration; therefore, my duty to you is complete. I insist that we return home now."

He studied her as if he couldn't quite figure her out. "As you wish, Your Highness." He remained still while the park servant locked the gate leading to the footpath.

The instant the man was gone from view, Zack's arm circled the princess's waist as he scooped her off her feet. In one quick movement, he hoisted her over the gate, then followed, never letting go of her arm.

"You insist on going home?" he snarled. "Well, fine, we'll go home. But *first,* you and I are going for a midnight hike."

28

Living Cam's Nightmare

∾

Zack kept a firm grip on Quinn's elbow, forcing her down the footpath.

Lamps along the way clicked off, leaving only the full moon to light the path. Even so, the princess stumbled from Zack's urgency.

Royal training had ingrained in her that one held a pleasant disposition and a mild manner at all times. Yet even the most mild-mannered princess could bear only so much. Zack had pushed her to the limit. She'd maintained her pleasant disposition far too long.

The crimes he'd already committed against Mandria's princess would cost him his head on the castle green—if the king ever got hold of him.

Digging her heels into the ground, Quinn stopped as stubbornly as a tunnel donkey.

"Where are you taking me?" she demanded, jerking her arm from his grasp.

"To the wishing pool." He grabbed her shoulder to make sure she stayed put. "I know that the pool has something to do with your power."

Oh, Sarah, why did you tell him of the pool?

The princess feigned exasperation. "Do you not listen? I do not have any sort of magic power. I am merely a normal . . ." She did not want to give him any more information than he already knew.

"A normal what?" He tilted his head as if trying to guess what she'd been about to say. "You may not possess magical powers, but you have an unusual ring. I've seen it." The lad took hold of her arms and jerked her hands from the shadows into the moonlight.

"Hey, it's gone. Where'd you hide it? You were wearing it when we left the school."

She refused to answer. What could she say? He was correct.

Taking hold of her shoulders, he gave her a frustrated shake.

"You're hurting me!" she cried, forgetting to control the anger flooding through her. Tears came into her eyes from the pain he was inflicting.

"I don't *care* if I'm hurting you," he said through clenched teeth. "You might as well tell me how to do the magic. I'm not taking you home until you do."

Quinn struggled, but he held on tightly, his fingers digging into her shoulders.

"Toads and mugwort!" she yelped, kicking him hard in the leg.

Startled by the kick and the unusual curse, Zack loosened his grip and swore at her.

Twisting away from him, she ran, gathering her billowing skirts to keep from tripping. Moonlight made the path easy to follow, but it also illuminated every hiding place.

Zack's heavy footfalls pounded after her.

Terrified, Quinn realized she should have broken her honorable agreement and gone home with Sarah and Scott when she had the chance. Proper Mandrian behavior was not serving the princess well in this world. Staying at WonderLand had been a foolish decision, yet she did not realize it at the time. She never dreamed Zack would harm her.

He'll do anything to get the magic.

Quinn stifled her thoughts—or *were* they her thoughts? Maybe Melikar was planting a warning in her mind. Was she truly in danger?

Her heartbeat matched her racing footfalls. A rustling in the trees along the path began to distract her as she ran. A slight tingle traveled through her.

The trees! They seemed to be reaching out their branches to her. Was the surrounding ·magic still strong enough to wake the wood nymphs? Were they trying to help? Trying to hinder her pursuer?

Behind her, she heard a few yelps and curses. *Yes! The dryads must be causing branches to bend low enough to block the path.*

Afraid to dare a chance by slowing to look behind and confirm her assumption, the princess kept on running. Why hadn't she worn the sturdy canvas shoes Adam had purchased for her? Jeweled Mandrian slippers were not meant for racing.

Her chest ached as though she'd swallowed a knight's dagger.

In spite of the obstacles, Zack was gaining on her. He played sports; he was good at running. And, unfortunately, the unusual action of the surrounding tree branches would only assure him that he was correct about her possession of some sort of magic.

The forest gave way to a moon-washed clearing. Quinn panicked at the thought of leaving the enchanted trees behind. But the path kept going, so she did, too, frantically searching for a place to hide.

Then she saw it. The path wound down a sloping hill to a footbridge, curving over a river, with a wide, still pool in the middle. On either side of the bridge, moonlight glinted off the water.

Terror pushed the princess down the path. She rushed straight toward the wishing pool. All she wanted was to be home and safe—and as far from Zack as she could get.

She wanted to be warm again, wanted to curl up with Scrabit and hide from the heartbreaking truths she'd learned today.

She wanted her mother and father.

She wanted Cam and Ameka.

Even so, a desire stronger than her own safety took hold of her as she ran. She wanted to protect her kingdom and its people.

She, the Royal Princess of Mandria, would give her life to guard the secret of her kingdom's existence.

And Adam? She must protect him, too. Protect him from Hannah's pain, and herself from Mondo's.

"Help me, Cam!" she cried as she ran. "I wish with all my heart to come home!"

As she shouted the words, she touched her finger, feeling for the ring. With a pang of regret, she remembered it was gone.

She was powerless.

Why hadn't she stopped Zack with the magic and worried later about consequences? She'd always been so quick to use the ring before.

Now it was too late.

Frantic, she could think of only one thing to do.

Reaching the footbridge, she bounded upon it, lifted herself onto the handrail, then paused to glance back, gasping for breath.

Zack raced toward the bridge. "What are you doing?" he shouted. "Stop!"

Quinn took a deep breath and closed her eyes. "Melikar, please, please let me come home."

Gathering her skirts, she jumped off the railing into the dark, moon-dappled water of the wishing pool.

29

Terror on the Footbridge

~

Quinn's face came out of the water.

Gasping for breath, she shoved hair from her face. Why had she gotten wet this time?

The princess opened her eyes, eager for a glimpse of Melikar's chamber. What she saw was Zack, hanging over the railing of the footbridge, mouth gaping as he stared at her.

"What are you trying to do? Kill yourself?" Hustling off the bridge to the bank of the river, he tried to grab hold of her without getting wet.

Arms flailing, Quinn pushed away from him, fighting to keep her face above the water and catch her breath.

Why am I still here?

Why do coins fall through the enchanted pool, but people do not?

She'd wanted dearly to believe that the choice to travel between worlds was her own. The shock of being wrong choked her with terror.

Without the ring, I cannot go home.

The princess sputtered and kicked, legs tangling in her skirts. A strangling sensation consumed her chest.

Ay, returning to Mandria is not my choice after all.

She'd tried twice—once, on the steps of the apartment with the ring, and now through the pool.

The princess gulped a mouthful of murky water. Not going back and not being *able* to go back were two different matters.

Mondo's words filtered into her mind: *"After the spell wore off, it was too late to return."*

Have I waited too long?

She needed air, yet her arms grew tired of pushing water away from her face. Despair overcame her. Drowsiness softened the panic.

What went wrong, Cam? My traveling here alone and staying was never part of our plan.

Maybe this was all a dream, and she'd awaken in her own sleeping chamber. Cydlin and Gwynell would be lighting the morning candles, and Scrabit—

Rushing water flooded her ears as she was rudely yanked from the river. Zack carried her over the muddy bank and up the curve of the footbridge, dropping her without gentleness.

He gave her an angry shake, yelling words that melted away before she could understand them. Kneeling, he covered her lips with his, blowing air into her mouth.

His actions startled and revived her. He was the *last* person in either world she wanted to kiss. Squirming away, she struggled to her feet, swinging both fists at him.

He caught her arms and pinned them to her sides. "I was trying to *help* you. Stop acting like this and give me what I want. Hand over the ring and tell me how it works. Then I'll let you go."

Soaked to the skin, Quinn began to shiver. Her gown, heavy with water, weighed her down.

Disgusted, Zack fumbled with her pockets. "Where have you hidden it?" he rasped, scattering a useless handful of color pots across the bridge.

"Don't!" Quinn cried, scrambling to recover her possessions. Stuffing them back into her pocket, she yelled at him, "I told you I don't *have* a magic ring!"

"Magic?" He narrowed his eyes at her. "I never called it a *magic* ring."

Moonshadows gave his grin a contorted wickedness.

Quinn glared at him, distracted by whispers poking at the back of her mind. She tried to ignore them.

"Remember," spoke a voice—or was it Cam's voice?

Blossoming in her mind was an image of her trip into this world: *Cam. The spell. The swirling water.*

"Listen to me!" Zack shouted, inches from her face. "If I don't get what I want, somebody's gonna get hurt."

"Remember" pounded with every beat of the princess's heart.

Her teeth began to chatter. If she did not get warm

soon, she feared she'd freeze to death.

Remember.

The words! The words to the spell.

Cam had been mumbling. No—she could not blame him. She *knew* the words—they were burned into her heart. But she was too upset to recall them right now. It was not fair.

Remember.

Zack ripped off his vest, flinging it onto the bridge. "I've had it with your little act of innocence. You're hiding the ring, and I'm going to find it."

The hatred glinting in his eyes horrified the princess. She shrank back, truly fearing the menacing lad.

"Help me, Cam!"

Her scream made Zack falter. He looked about to see who she was talking to.

Had she said the words out loud?

REMEMBER.

Cam!

Zack lunged at her, ripping the front of her gown.

She fought him with all her strength, while the voice inside her head *almost* told her what to do. But not quite.

Quinn pushed away.

Zack flipped her around, hurting her.

Then he yanked her against him to make her stop moving.

She stepped around him to keep from tripping over his feet.

Around.

Yes! That is what she needed to remember. Around . . .

The princess repeated the motion. A soft stirring of water teased her ears. The water in the wishing pool was moving! Had she caused it? Had she triggered the spell the way Cam's stirring of the cauldron did?

If so, it was her only hope. Yanking herself free of Zack, the princess began to twirl by herself.

The lad seized her again.

Clutching Zack's arms, she forced him to turn with her.

"What the—?" He shoved her away, as if she'd suddenly gone mad.

Quinn twirled again and again, wet skirts flapping against her legs.

Ignoring Zack, she crossed her arms over her heart and squeezed her eyes shut to concentrate on Mandria. On home.

I wish it with all of my heart.

Enchantment trembled through her body, rumbling to her very core, like earthquakes beneath the river.

Darkness claimed every corner of her mind.

Her last thought was of Adam.

30

The Tapestry
Is Unwoven

Midnight dawned into morning, slowly, the way daylight crept through windows in the apartment.

The princess's head filled with cottony clouds from the blue skies of Outer Earth. As the mist cleared, she felt gentle arms encircling her, holding her.

"Adam," she mumbled. "You found me."

The clouds melted.

The princess opened her eyes. She was lying on a cobblestone floor.

Cam knelt beside her, his arms enfolding her.

Quinn's heart leaped with an equal mixture of surprise, relief, and happiness.

"Cam!"

Looking as if he'd seen a departed spirit, the apprentice released her from his embrace and shot to his feet.

"I—I beg your royal pardon."

He bowed his head, but the princess could tell he was grinning.

She struggled to get up, so Cam gingerly assisted her.

Ignoring her torn, wet gown, the princess flung her arms around the lad's neck. "I am home!" She noticed how trembly and weak her voice sounded, yet it also sounded more familiar with walls all around to echo it back to her. The way it always sounded in Mandria.

Cautiously, the apprentice returned the hug, still grinning. "Welcome home, Princess," he whispered. "I—we've missed you. You've worried us so."

As Quinn's mind cleared, the realization of events returned in a rush.

Pulling away from Cam, she peered up through the wishing pool.

The water was slowly settling into stillness. The moon's brightness filtered through the pool, making a pale circle on the floor of Melikar's chamber.

A lone figure paced atop the bridge, agitated, stopping every other step to stare into the pool.

Quinn's heart shrank. She had failed to uphold all of the Mandrian truths. "Now Zack knows."

"No," came a sharp voice from the shadows. Melikar stepped into the moon circle, mumbling a spell beneath his breath.

He raised one arm, making a series of quick gestures, then spoke calmly, "The lad with wicked intent shall never recall what has taken place. He will have no memory of the ring nor of Mandria's princess."

Quinn squinted through the pool again. Zack stopped pacing. Glancing at his surroundings, he acted disoriented, then snatched up his vest and disappeared off the footbridge.

The wizard lowered his arm and faced her.

Quinn tried to read the expression on his face—a blend of anger and relief.

"Oh, Melikar." She threw herself into his robed arms, startling the old enchanter.

Hugging was not royal protocol, but she did not care; she'd *never* cared for royal protocol. "I am sorry I displeased you, Sire. Forgive me."

Melikar gently took hold of her shoulders. "The tapestry has been unwoven in the evil lad's mind; the damage, reversed. I will cast another spell upon the Dover lad and maiden to erase all remembrance of Mandria and you from their minds."

His words were daggers piercing her heart.

Melikar closed his eyes, mumbling the chant once more.

The thought of living her life obsessed with the memory of Adam, yet knowing he would not recall a single hair of her tresses was more than Quinn could bear.

"No!" She thrust her hand to cover the wizard's lips. "Melikar, I beg you in the name of the High Spirit."

The enchanter pushed her hand away, slowly beginning the gesture. "The maiden, Sarah, has now forgotten."

Tears streaked Quinn's cheeks. "Please do not take the memory of me from Adam. How can you be so cruel?" She pounded her fists against the wizard's chest in a weak attempt to stop him. "I command you!"

Her own words appalled her. The princess had never used her royal status over Melikar's judgments, always bowing to his authority. Yet it wasn't a true command from the throne—merely empty words spoken in desperation. She knew that he knew the same.

The wizard placed a firm hand on Quinn's head, tilting it backward, locking gazes with her. His translucent eyes shimmered in fiery bursts of red.

The princess held her breath, unable to tear her gaze away from his. Quivers shuddered through her as though the wizard's eyes burned into her very soul, reading words written in her deepest heart.

Melikar's eyes flashed to normal as he released his grip. Lifting his hand, he resumed the chant. "The young lad—"

The princess slumped to the floor, sobbing.

"—will always remember."

She raised her tear-smudged face to the old wizard. Without speaking a word, she thanked him from her deepest heart.

He acknowledged her silent gratitude. A tender smile twitched the edge of his mustache as he helped the princess to her feet. "All others, except Mondo, shall forget."

Bowing her head, the princess accepted his decision.

"Cam," Melikar ordered. "Come here."

The apprentice, who had witnessed the scene from the shadows with much curiosity and consternation, sprang forward at the command.

"Prepare the antidote for doleran seeds at once."

Cam rushed to do the enchanter's bidding.

"Princess, return to your chamber for a dry gown. Your ladies will be bursting with questions. Answer whatever you wish, for the instant you are properly dressed and coifed, they will view you as you have always been and shall not recall your absence. Go about the rest of your evening as though nothing has been amiss."

Pausing, he touched one hand to his forehead and mumbled a chant. "Upon the awakening of the king and queen, the royal attendants will have no remembrance of the lost time or their idle hours."

Suddenly the portal burst open.

Ameka dashed in, pulled by a dragon on a leash. "I was taking Scrabit for a walk, and I—" Her fluttering gaze fell upon the disheveled princess. "Oh, glory!"

The two maidens rushed toward each other, then stopped.

Quinn, foregoing royal protocol once more, hugged her surprised tutor as she would have hugged a friend in the other world. Then she gave her pet dragon a good scratching on his scaly neck.

Melikar ignored the gaiety, somberly closing the door.

The three gathered near to hear his words.

"My children," he began, "the kingdom of Mandria

will go on the way it has for countless generations. No one shall mention the disappearance of its princess this quarter-moon's turn. The secret must remain in your hearts."

As if on cue, they all shared the Sign of the Lorik.

Quinn's heart split in two, contemplating those cherished most dearly. She had not realized how much Mandria meant to her until it opened its bosom and pulled her home.

Yet part of her remembered another old man she'd grown fond of, the sister she'd never had, and one whose image was too painful to call to memory right now.

She'd think of Adam later. She'd write of him in her journal—

Ay, I left the journal behind. I shall have to start anew.

The princess slipped her hand into the pocket of her gown, making sure *something* from the other world remained. Her fingers curled around the color pots and the lash tint, bringing a smile to her face. To compensate for losing all else, she would proudly walk her kingdom's tunnels with darkened lashes and sun-kissed cheeks.

Melikar opened his great robed arms, collecting his Mandrian followers. Forming a circle, symbol of eternity, they clasped wrists while Melikar, their loyal wizard, proclaimed the newest Mandrian truth:

"The princess from under the river has come home."

Epilogue

$\mathcal{A}$dam trudged the footpath through the forest at WonderLand Park, head bowed, shoulders hunched.

The princess was gone.

She hadn't come home last night, so he'd gone out searching for her. She wasn't anywhere he could think to look. And when he'd run into Zack early this morning at the track and started yelling at him, Zack had no idea what Adam was talking about. He could tell Zack wasn't faking—he really had no clue who Quinn was or where she was.

The princess must have returned to her kingdom. Yet how could she leave after all they'd told each other?

And how could she leave without saying good-bye?

Adam thought of their last precious moments together. If he knew he would never see her again, he'd have thought it a fitting good-bye.

Never see her again.

The words ripped his heart. He'd forever be haunted by what she had started to tell him when Zack interrupted them.

Adam stepped from the trees into the clearing and headed toward the wishing pool. The water was calm and still, despite a crisp wind stirring golden leaves in the overhanging branches. Quinn had told him of the spell Melikar cast to keep their window to this world always clear.

Climbing the curve of the footbridge, he sank to his knees, peering into the blue-green pool.

Are you there? Will I ever see you again?

Adam touched the magic ring on his finger, wishing with all his heart for the princess to appear.

He waited.

Nothing happened.

Touching the ring once more, he wished her his love. *My heart embraces you.*

A gust of wind blew a bedraggled flower against his knee. Adam picked up the blue rose he'd woven into Quinn's braid the night before.

Plucking the petals, he dropped them into the wishing pool, one by one.

What happens next?

Will the princess ever see Adam again?

Will Cam's magic ever be strong enough
to cast a proper spell?

Will the secret of Mandria's existence be revealed?

The story of the princess and the wizard's
apprentice continues in

Cam's Quest

Peril lies ahead, and peril lies behind . . .